A Holiday Engagement

M.A. Nichols

Books by M.A. Nichols

Generations of Love Series

The Kingsleys

Flame and Ember

Hearts Entwined

A Stolen Kiss

The Ashbrooks

A True Gentleman

The Shameless Flirt

A Twist of Fate

The Honorable Choice

The Finches

The Jack of All Trades

Tempest and Sunshine

The Christmas Wish

The Leighs

An Accidental Courtship

Love in Disguise

His Mystery Lady

A Debt of Honor

Christmas Courtships

A Holiday Engagement
Beneath the Mistletoe

Standalone Romances

Honor and Redemption
A Tender Soul
A Passing Fancy
To Have and to Hold

Fantasy Novels

The Villainy Consultant Series

Geoffrey P. Ward's Guide to Villainy
Geoffrey P. Ward's Guide to Questing
Magic Slippers: A Novella

The Shadow Army Trilogy

Smoke and Shadow
Blood Magic
A Dark Destiny

Table of Contents

Chapter 1

Christmas Eve 1820
Bristow, Essex

"Did you spy Mrs. Hensen's gown?" said Mama, leaning closer to Mrs. Ellis with her fan held before her mouth as though to muffle her question. The lady would've done better not to speak at all, for no amount of wood and lace could mute her words when spoken at that volume. "My goodness, what is the point of coming to a ball if one does not attempt to look one's best?"

Mrs. Thompson and Mrs. Ellis tittered, that brittle sound grating like metal against metal.

"I think the color is becoming on her," said Charity Baxter, but Mama and her friends only huffed at that and circled closer as they picked apart the details of Mrs. Hensen's coiffure and toilette, devouring each morsel like the vultures they were.

Beside them, Mrs. Ingalls and another circle of ladies stiffened at the stream of venom, for Mama never regulated her tone, speaking as though sharing a secret but delivering it loudly enough for anyone to overhear it. Charity tried to catch Mrs. Ingalls' eye, as though a shared wince might offer enough of an apology, but the ladies of Bristow knew better than to look directly at the Baxters, for it might attract a predator. If only they knew Mrs. Baxter and her ilk were scavengers and were scared easily by anyone stronger than them.

Instead, Mrs. Ingalls and her group scurried to another corner of the ballroom, as though that might protect them from Mama's biting words. Charity let out a low breath, her shoulders lowering as she stood there, not knowing what to do with herself. But when Mama began mocking poor Mrs. Wilson, Charity couldn't remain there any longer. Mama was so preoccupied with her tirade about the poor widow's newly reduced circumstances that she didn't notice her daughter drifting away from her side, though Charity couldn't breathe properly until she was hidden amongst the other guests.

Lingering at the edge of the dance floor, she studied the people around her, searching for any friendly port in the storm. The others kept their backs firmly to Charity, and even those merely passing by stepped clear, making certain that not even their skirts brushed hers, though the crowd was packed tightly.

Miss Stowe stood to one side, her hands clasped before her as she watched the dancers, her face so full of longing that Charity practically heard her thoughts shouting for the nearby gentlemen to ask her to stand up with her.

Straightening her shoulders, she drew up beside Miss Stowe. "I adore this song, don't you?"

The young lady made a good show of it, holding fast to decorum and allowing her eyes to widen only a fraction before greeting her with a nod, but Miss Stowe couldn't hide the fear glinting in her gaze or the stiffness of her posture. Charity affected a smile, giving her best attempt at casual ease, but Miss Stowe only tensed further.

"Does your family have any favorite traditions this time of year?" It was the first thing Charity could think to ask; though rarely an interesting subject, people enjoyed speaking of themselves.

Miss Stowe remained frozen in place, blinking, and Charity

held onto her friendly expression, but it had little effect. The pair stared at each other until Charity finally sighed and looked away. As though breaking the spell, Miss Stowe mumbled something about her mother needing her and hurried away, much in the same fashion Mrs. Ingalls had fled from Mama.

Taking a deep breath, Charity remained in place, gazing at the ballroom as though nothing were amiss. However, she felt a hint of Miss Stowe's desperation seeping into her heart as she searched the crowd for any sign of welcome.

To one side stood the new Mrs. Thackeray, holding court with a group of ladies all about Charity's age. The circle of ladies looked as bright as the chandelier above them; not in a physical sense, but something inside them shone, their faces alight with the thrill of the Christmas Eve party, the conversation sparkling between them as they laughed. Charity felt as though sequestered in the dark corner of the room, shrouded and out of sight. For the briefest of moments, she considered joining them, but with each heartbeat, that sad organ sank lower in her chest as the truth of the situation settled once more on her shoulders, clearing away the fantasies she'd harbored.

Tonight would be no different from the rest. How many times must she throw herself on society's mercy before she finally accepted the truth? Charity Baxter had no place in society. Not anymore.

The Twelve Days of Christmas were a time of frivolity. As though laughing in the face of the dark and cold, people opened their homes and hearts, filling them with light. Parties, feasts, dancing, and merriment filled every waking hour. Families and friends gathered round the proverbial hearth, basking in the warmth of brotherhood and kinship. They drank too much, ate too much, and reveled in the generosity of those around them while giving back in equal abundance.

It was a time of renewal and rebirth. Where they bid farewell to the old and welcomed the new. Shedding the heartaches of the previous year to usher in the next, full of hope and promise.

But for Charity Baxter, it was a bitter reminder of the past, a mockery of the present, and a sign that life would continue its present course, stretching on from one year to the next in the same unending mix of discomfort, ennui, and irritation until the sweet release of death brought about a new life. Hopefully, a better one.

Charity let out a heavy sigh. She was being maudlin. It did no good to wallow in such disheartening thoughts, but sometimes one longed to roll about in it like a pig in mud. There was little point in being optimistic about her future when the New Year had no power to alter her course, and her present trajectory ensured the coming twelve months were likely to be worse than the twelve before it.

And attempting to enliven her spirits during a ball was impossible. While most might believe such festivities were a perfect distraction from dreary reality, her troubles stemmed from the people in this room. At least at home, Charity could hide in her bedchamber and pretend this world didn't exist, rather than having her nose rubbed in it.

At least Mama and Papa did not drag them to Bath for the Season any longer; a younger Charity would've found that intolerable, but now that she was well past her maidenly prime and nipping at the heels of thirty, she couldn't imagine anything more dreadful than being forced to traipse about Bath, filling her time with the pointlessness of society. Vacuous fools.

But there was no avoiding Bristow society at this time of year.

Charity took a fortifying breath. Twelve days. That was all. Surely, she could survive this. She simply needed to keep her mind away from the past. Perhaps the present wouldn't be so bad if she did not compare it with what had been, but that required more fortitude and self-control than Charity possessed. And with nothing else to occupy her attention, it was little wonder that her mind drifted back to the days when she'd been the epicenter of Bristow's society.

Standing at the edge of the ballroom, Charity steeled her

nerves and pretended to study the decorations. The truly fashionable wouldn't deign to give the sparse adornments more than a passing glance. The Assembly rooms were, in a word, plain, and Mrs. Thompson had done little to enhance the space. Though the rich grain of the walls was lovely, the dark wood snuffed out all the light, and their hosts' stingy budget hadn't allowed for the army of candles required to properly illuminate the space. So, it was wise of them not to neglect the decorations, for they were difficult to see in any detail.

The Thompsons attempted to compensate for such deficiencies with an overabundance of entertainment and refreshments. Some guests indulged in cards, others in parlor games, whilst many availed themselves of the massive amounts of mediocre food that was good for staving off starvation but little else. At least the musicians were talented, but then, they were the ones Mama had deemed the proper players for such an event; the lady may be a shrew of the highest order, but she had good taste.

Charity frowned at herself. She was in a mood, which was made all the worse when she spied the Thompsons' string of yule candles burning in the windows, serving as a reminder that there was none to be found in the Baxters' home. Merchants were not keen to give such gifts to those with unpaid bills.

Shaking away those feelings, she skirted the edge of the ballroom, her gaze fixed on the evergreen boughs that surrounded the musicians' dais. They circled the edge and climbed the wall in such a thick burst of needles that Charity wondered if Mrs. Thompson had placed it there in hopes of hiding the players; the lady had often bemoaned that the room had no nook in which to hide the musicians, but all their hostess had done was to highlight their place at the far end of the room.

With her gaze fixed on the decorations, Charity sauntered around the edge of the ballroom, refusing to look at anyone lest they believe her to be begging for a partner (though she was doing precisely that). Her feet itched to dance. To do something—anything—to free her of this melancholy.

But that hope died when the Kingsleys strode into the ball.

Mrs. Mina Kingsley held her husband's arm, beaming and nodding at the crowd like a fairy princess deigning to visit this mortal realm, gifting the lowly people with her beneficence. And that man. Mr. Simon Kingsley looked like the vacuous fool he was, gazing at the world around him but unable to comprehend any of it.

In all honesty, Charity wondered why Mrs. Kingsley put up with the twit. Of course, if the rumors were true, the lady had abandoned him for a time in the first months of their marriage, but Charity couldn't verify that tidbit. Nor did it matter, for Mrs. Kingsley was there now, standing at her husband's side.

Avoiding them altogether was impossible, but they were not friends with the Thompsons, and Charity ought to have been saved from this discomfort tonight. Yet, there they were. The Kingsleys meandered through the crowd, and though she tried to force her attention away, Charity tracked every movement. It wasn't as though she mourned the loss of that man, specifically, but it was impossible not to feel her spirits sink at the sight of what might've been.

Dear heavens, she was being ridiculously morose this evening. Charity took a deep breath, filling her lungs before letting it out in a long, cleansing sigh.

"My, my, that was a sad sound."

Charity turned to see a frock coat that had the power to make ladies swoon with delight; the rich blue resembled the deepest depths of the ocean, and the gold buttons sparkled against the darkness, twinkling like stars. The splice of his white waistcoat was pristine, contrasting even more beside the frock coat; clearly, this was the stranger's dress uniform, for it showed little of the wear and tear one expected of the navy.

Having once fallen prey to the navy fever that gripped so many young ladies, Charity recognized the details that marked this gentleman as a lieutenant. What she didn't know was his name, for she was certain she had never clapped eyes on the man before: his face was far too appealing to forget.

Clearly no longer in his youth, Charity guessed the gentleman was in his thirties. His strong features would look dark and brooding if not for the dimples and grin resting easily on his face, and his stark black hair seemed caught in a perpetual breeze, pushing back from his face as though he had just stepped off the deck of his ship. His physique showed the signs of his active profession, though without the bulk and imposing air of a bruiser. From tip to toe, the stranger was every bit the adventurous mariner, and his light blue eyes sparked with laughter as he accepted her study of him.

Lips pinched, Charity stiffened and turned her attention back to the decorations (poor though they may be). Irritation was far preferable to melancholy, and she welcomed it with open arms. Impertinent man.

Chapter 2

"And why is such a pretty lady standing by herself?" he asked, coming to stand beside her.

Charity frowned, her spine straightening as she refused to allow her eyes to drift toward the lieutenant. With a tone as frigid as the winter wind outside, she replied, "I do not believe we are acquainted, sir."

That tone ought to bring the man to his senses, but when he answered, the stranger's tone was thick with laughter. "And that is why I am standing here—to make your acquaintance."

Nostrils flaring, Charity took another deep breath. Mockery. She was well familiar with it, though few were ever as bold as this.

"As I was invited to this private gathering, it presupposes that our host and hostess do not consider me a nave," he added. "That ought to be endorsement enough."

Charity bit back a retort, refusing to look at him, though from the corner of her eye, she saw him tuck his hands behind him as though settling in for a good coze. She took yet another restorative breath, but it did not lighten her mood for her muscles refused to relax.

"Or are the Thompsons the sort to invite rogues and rascals to their gatherings?" he asked.

Scowling, Charity huffed. "Of course not, sirrah. But a lady has few powers in this world, and the ability to choose her acquaintances is amongst them. Once an introduction is made, it cannot be undone, and a gentleman mustn't spring upon her and force her into such an uncomfortable situation. I know nothing of your character, except for the behavior you display at present, which doesn't recommend you."

But rather than looking properly cowed, the Lieutenant beamed, his blue eyes alight with mischief. "And now that you've deigned to acknowledge me, might you give me your name?"

Charity's gaze jerked away, her teeth grinding together. "And what would you do with it?"

"How am I to ask you to dance if I do not know it?"

That drew her eyes right back to the bounder, and for all that Charity knew better than to show weakness, she couldn't help the furrow of her brow or the gaping of her mouth. Perhaps she ought to have predicted the Lieutenant's motive (and the Charity-that-Was would've anticipated just such a thing), but it had been some time since a gentleman sought her company. But then, the townsfolk knew her history.

Gathering her composure in a trice, Charity returned her gaze to the dancers. "Does dancing require names?"

"I suppose not," he replied, and then came to stand before her, sweeping into a low bow. "My dear mystery lady, wouldst thou do me the honor of attending me for a set?"

A cold current swept through her veins. More mockery. It felt as though the world were pressing down on her, gravity's pull now stronger than before, but Charity held onto her composure, forcing her shoulders up. Her chest tightened as she realized the truth of the matter. Jest or not, she would accept. Her feet itched to dance and lose herself in the music and steps, ignoring the world as it was and reveling in a fantasy.

With a man who was only using her to amuse himself.

Was she that desperate? The sinking of her stomach attested to the truth. Charity Baxter was, indeed, that undiscerning—pathetic creature that she was. But that did not mean she would allow Lieutenant Whatever-His-Name to twit her any further.

Holding out her hand, Charity allowed him to lead her into the dance. With determined steps, she kept her head high and her gaze fixed on their destination, ignoring the others around them. Inserting themselves into the line, Charity hardly missed a beat as they took their place. The light, skipping steps came easily as they moved through the promenades and poussettes, each couple casting off in turn.

But as they progressed to the next position, Charity noticed a lady three couples down snickering while leaning close to whisper to a gentleman as they crossed. Her gaze darted to Charity and back, as though attempting to be subtle in her attentions. And failing, of course. How else would their victim know she was the object of their ridicule if not by feigning embarrassment at being "caught?"

Charity squared her shoulders, but the magic of the dance dissipated when others took up the jest. Perhaps it was merely her imagination, but it felt as though the entire ballroom rang with laughter directed at her.

That is the lady whom Simon Kingsley abandoned in favor of a marriage of convenience to a dowdy spinster. How horrid must she be for him to have chosen a stranger over a young lady of beauty and standing in the community? A lady like Mina Ashbrook? Positively ghastly...

She'd heard so many subtle and none-too-subtle variations of those speculations in the nine years since Mr. Kingsley's marriage. Ignoring them (or attempting to), Charity moved through the steps, her feet flitting through the dance with little trouble. Though the same could not be said of her partner.

He stumbled. And not once. She knew it was unlikely the Lieutenant had practiced much aboard a ship, and the *Duke of Wellington's Visit to Bath* was a new country dance. However, the steps were not complicated, and others called out the movements. Yet still, the Lieutenant tripped over his own feet. Surely, a man who navigated a rocking ship was sure-footed.

For not the first time in her life, Charity sent out a prayer of gratitude that she was blessed with a clear complexion. An artful blush was a strong tool to have in one's flirtation arsenal, but that also led to one's cheeks flushing red in embarrassment, which only added to the discomfort of the moment; no one needed to see her unease as she moved through the steps.

Charity ignored everyone—including her bungling partner. But luck did not favor her, and their part came to a rest, giving them a brief respite in which they stood on either side of the line, facing each other. She tried not to stare, but he showed no such good breeding (why she was surprised, she didn't know).

"What has brought you to Bristow?" Though Charity wasn't interested in the answer, it seemed the proper thing to ask at that time and a better course of action than merely staring at each other.

"I am visiting a naval friend," he replied. "I'm stuck ashore through January."

Gracious! Charity forced herself not to balk at that revelation. Though she couldn't count every member of the gentry amongst her acquaintances, Bristow's society was not so vast that there was another naval officer in the area. This infuriating Lieutenant was Mr. Graham Ashbrook's guest. A friend to Simon Kingsley's brother-in-law, in fact. She held back a scoff and wondered if the Lieutenant's host knew he was dancing with the devil.

"You didn't wish to spend your limited time ashore at home?" she asked, her voice as unsmiling as her expression.

The Lieutenant gave her a grin that she supposed was intended to be saucy or flirtatious or some other equally ridiculous thing. "Why go somewhere old when I can visit somewhere new?"

Charity frowned as he dared to wink at her. Wink! As though they shared some great jest, though at present, the only thing humorous was that she was stuck at this man's side until the end of their set—and that was more of the bitter variety. Fate adored tormenting her.

The man was off-putting. Charity couldn't help but feel that he was playacting. Though that wasn't it. She shook her head at herself as she tried to give a name to her unsettled feeling. But what did it matter? She'd spent a lifetime amongst the society serpents, who were as sincere and warm as the first of their kind, who'd tempted Eve to partake of the forbidden fruit. Feigned kindness and humor were prized among that set, and Charity had no patience for it any longer.

Squaring her shoulders, she ignored her partner as they were thrown into another round, moving through the progressions while she turned her thoughts away from anything but the lively music, the skipping steps, and the joy of the dance. The notes flowed through her, sweeping her feet along as the world faded into nothing, erasing everything but that which brought light and happiness. Perhaps she could remain there—

"Am I to assume I am dancing with the town pariah?" asked the Lieutenant, ripping her from her daydreams.

Charity let out a sharp breath.

"There is that sigh again," he said with a smirk.

"Yes, that is bound to happen when one is being constantly tormented," she muttered, and when he asked her to repeat herself, Charity waved it away.

"With so many snickers sent your direction, I have to assume I'm standing up with either someone of dubious reputation." His voice dropped low on the two words, dousing them with heavy-handed humor. "For all that you were worried about me forcing my questionable association on you, perhaps I ought to have asked around about you first. I would hate to be the known acquaintance of a corrupting influence."

Charity's teeth ground together as his mockery rang through her. There was something so flippant in his tone that she knew the Lieutenant did not expect a serious answer, and so she gave it.

"Indeed, I am the town pariah."

The Lieutenant scoffed—he actually scoffed!—and then laughed as though it was the best of jests.

"And what have you done to earn such scorn?" he asked with another one of his infuriating smirks. Charity wondered if he would still smile if she belted him. A man of the navy surely could not fault her for resorting to fisticuffs to settle a battle, but this was a different sort of engagement—not one settled with rifles and swords but with words and manners. And the lieutenant was a fool of the highest order if he thought he would best her.

Turning a serene smile to him, Charity gave him a flutter of her lashes. "It is because I'm standing up with the village idiot."

The Lieutenant let out a great bark of laughter, ringing out over the sound of the musicians and drawing quite a bit of attention.

Though Charity had been jesting (if only partly), her insinuation seemed apt enough for the gentleman (if she could even call him such) constantly made light of everything. If the Lieutenant had any thoughts in his head (and Charity seriously doubted he did), they were unlikely to be anything of substance. No, he spent his time amusing himself at others' expense.

The vapid, self-serving twit! Village idiot, indeed.

Chapter 3

A ball was a useless affair. Whether held in the height of the holidays with all the extra trimmings or in a friend's parlor with a smattering of couples, Thomas Callaghan thought the whole thing ridiculous. The music and movement distracted from the conversation and added to an overall air of anticipation between bachelors and maidens that would never be fulfilled. How many romantic dreams would die tonight? Or evaporate with the rising sun?

When Graham Ashbrook had insisted they attend this farce, Thomas had anticipated an entirely dreary evening when fate had dropped this bit of fun in his lap. So to speak. By Jove, this lady was quite entertaining.

She had all the bearing of a queen, deigning to bless her serfs with her presence, carrying herself with such haughtiness that it was no real sport to tease her, for she rose to every bait, getting more flustered and furious with each word. Miss Mystery had quite the tongue and enough mettle to let it loose, and Thomas attempted to hide his laughter, but it was no use. Captain McGregor was quite right; Thomas had no sense of self-preservation, but it was far too entertaining to fluster the lady.

Lips pursed and nose pointed high in the air, Miss Mystery

ignored him while skipping through the dance. For all her pretending, Thomas sensed she was keenly aware of his attention on her, and when her hazel eyes fell on him, they blazed, the green of her dress bringing that same shade out in her gaze.

With an exaggerated step, Thomas feigned a stumble and turned the wrong direction, earning him a few grumbles from the others and a burning glare from his partner. But her silence could only last so long. Soon, the dance deposited them opposite each other with a long stretch of nothing to do, and for all her haughtiness, Miss Mystery couldn't ignore him entirely when standing before her, staring at her.

Honestly, the lady was quite the puzzle. She had the air of one who ought to be knee-deep in the center of these festivities, surrounded by a circle of beaus who were wound around her finger. Though as she looked closer to thirty than twenty, he supposed she ought to be married off to some poor fool and commanding the attention of the other matrons.

With delicate features properly placed and proportioned, Miss Mystery was easily one of the loveliest ladies in the gathering (when she didn't insist on twisting them into a sour expression). And many a man would go to great lengths to secure a wife with her figure; even the columnar styles couldn't hide its perfection beneath the straight, drab lines.

Miss Mystery had all the makings of a belle, not a wallflower. Yet, it was clear from her solitary position where he'd found her and the incessant staring of those around them that she was anything but Society's Darling.

They were hardly admiring his fine dancing; Thomas made certain of that. If he didn't wish to be pressed into standing up with every dance, he needed to prove himself the highest level of dancing incompetent. A country dance dolt. A quadrille quack. And he was doing a splendid job of ensuring no one would wish to endure a set with him.

"And what have you done to earn their wrath?" Thomas couldn't help but ask the question, for it was certain to earn him more ire. And Miss Mystery didn't disappoint. That pert little nose turned upward, her ringlets bouncing as she turned her face away from him. She didn't go so far as to fold her arms, but dismissal radiated off her.

Challenge accepted. Thomas laughed to himself, imagining what Miss Mystery might say if properly riled.

"Did you steal the mayor's carriage? Spill punch all over his wife's gown? Snore loudly during Sunday services?" Then lowering his voice, Thomas leaned in and whispered, "Did you allow your spoon to clink against your teacup after supper?"

But that earned him no biting retort or blaze of fury. Thomas had anticipated Miss Mystery returning in kind, matching his ridiculousness with haughtiness, but the stiffness in her posture softened, her brows drawing close together as she truly seemed not to see him for the first time during their conversation.

"Once dethroned, one is hardly allowed to remain in a position of power," she said, her voice low enough that Thomas wasn't certain he'd heard her correctly.

"Ah, I see," he said with a broad grin. "Like Napoleon, you've been ousted and now live in exile. Banished to the social wastelands."

Miss Mystery's shoulders drew up once more, her eyes snapping to his. "And what does it matter to you?"

"I am just a traveler who enjoys spreading smiles wherever I go," he said with a waggle of his brows. "When I saw you standing there, alone, I couldn't help myself. I had to brighten your day."

Those hazel eyes held his, her expression relaxing into an inscrutable mask as Miss Mystery studied him for a long moment. "No, you are mocking me. Teasing and twitting me for your own amusement, giving no thought or care to my feelings. You are no better than the others, who do so from a distance. You are worse, in fact, for at least they allow me to find solace in my thoughts. You won't even allow me to enjoy this dance."

Thomas stilled, his smile falling as the past few minutes played back through his mind, searching for any defense he might mount against the accusation, but the fact that he had to search so thoroughly was answer enough. Shifting in place, he scratched at the back of his head, feeling like a lad being reprimanded before the class. Worse of all, he knew he deserved it.

It wasn't Miss Mystery's fault that he'd been dragged here this evening. Of course, it wasn't Ashbrook's either; Thomas was a grown man entirely capable of begging off. But before he could offer a word of apology, the blasted dance pulled them apart once more, and Miss Mystery ignored him once more.

Charity's limbs felt like lead, and all the joy of the dance leached out as she counted the steps that drew her closer to the end of this torture. Not that Mama would allow her to retreat home when there were so many hours yet to go. So, Charity occupied herself with planning escape routes. Their house wasn't so very far from here; if she slid out the side door, her mother mightn't even notice her missing until it was too late.

Straightening her spine, Charity ignored the others. Or told herself to do so. Such things were easier in theory than practice, and though she tried to slough off the snickers and laughter, it was impossible when she was dancing with their embodiment.

Would she forever be the butt of everyone's joke? The laughingstock of Bristow? Surrounded by people who had once claimed friendship but now mocked her every movement. Even strangers made an effort to tease and torment her, putting her on display as society's fool. Their unwitting jester.

Charity's lips trembled, and she fought against the feelings burbling to the surface, but her chin joined in, quivering as those thoughts weighed heavy on her shoulders, pressing down on her. Drawing in a deep breath, she forced those wretched tears aside and took her place across from the Lieutenant as the dance deposited her in purgatory once more.

But that satisfied smirk was absent from the Lieutenant's expression, replaced with something far worse. His brow wrinkled, his lips pursed, and even his head was cocked to the side in that same manner she'd seen so many times during the first assembly when Mr. Kingsley had foisted the new Mrs. Kingsley onto Bristow.

Charity straightened, drawing her head up high. "Do not pity me, sirrah. I may be the sad and lonely pariah, but at least I have the integrity to be what I am and not flounce around pretending I am something I am not."

"Pardon?" he asked, his brow furrowing.

"Do not feign ignorance again."

The Lieutenant's words played through her mind, each mocking tone reverberating through her and joining in with the others. The pressure in her chest grew, and though a sensible voice in her mind warned her to breathe, Charity couldn't pay it any mind, shoving it far away as heat burned through her.

"Yes, I am a curmudgeon, but what of it?" she asked, her chin jutting out. "At least I am honest. You laugh and smile, feigning a good nature while using others' foibles to feed your amusement. That is the worst sort of tormentor. They seem harmless with their sweet expressions and sugared words, but they cut deep into the heart of another, twisting the knife. And all the others applaud and join in, thinking it's jolly good fun, but it is disgusting."

Standing there like a gaping fool, Thomas had no idea what to say to such a thing. Of course, the lady did not allow him to gather his thoughts before launching into another tirade, and he could only stare as she scowled at him.

"You are fake, through and through, like all the rest, and I am done with pretending to be something I am not."

Thomas scoffed. "I am not playacting."

But she merely echoed his scoff. "Even your dancing is false, Lieutenant. It takes skill and grace to navigate the dance floor with so many missteps without losing the beat. And no crushed toes or torn flounces? Even mediocre dancers cannot manage such a feat. You are as genuine as glass beads claiming to be gems."

Continuing to gape at the lady, Thomas certainly hoped the natural tan of the naval man was dark enough to hide the flush of heat stealing across his cheeks.

"Miss—" But Thomas paused, not sure what to call her, for he knew using the appellate he'd dubbed her would hardly help matters.

"No," she said, shaking her head with a hard frown. "I am finished with false people. I've wasted too much of my life currying their favor, and I swore long ago not to play those games again."

Turning on her heel, Miss Mystery marched away, threading through the dancers and drawing a few huffs and frowns. And Thomas had no choice but to follow after her, though he had no thought as to what he could say after such an accusation.

"Miss—" Thomas cursed himself again, and doubly so when she paused at the edge of the dance floor and whirled on him.

"Do you wish to mock me further? You certainly do not desire my company for any genuine reasons, and your friends would not welcome a closer acquaintance."

"What do you mean?"

"Ask them, and I am certain they will enumerate my many sins. Ah, see!" said Miss Mystery, her eyes darting past Thomas to someone behind him. "Here he comes in all his righteous anger to warn you away from me, Lieutenant."

"I do not understand—" But Thomas's words were cut short at the sound of Ashbrook at his elbow.

"What is going on, Thomas?" However, his friend's steely gaze was fixed on Miss Mystery. Then with a cold tone, Ashbrook greeted her with a stilted, "Miss Baxter."

"Mr. Ashbrook," she replied with similar gusto before turning about and slipping away. Thomas stared after her, watching as she disappeared into the crowd.

"Simon and I were planning on a few rounds of cards, and we hoped you'd join us," said Ashbrook.

"Who was that?" asked Thomas, nodding in the direction

Miss Mystery had disappeared.

Ashbrook frowned. "Nothing good comes from the Baxters. Best to leave her be."

Affecting another cheeky grin, Thomas arched a brow. "You realize that makes her sound intriguing. Almost too alluring to ignore."

But that earned him no laugh and slap on the shoulder. "The Baxters are a wretched lot, and though Miss Baxter has fallen from grace, her mother is still a fixture of Bristow society and holds much power. They've caused my sister, my brother-in-law, and my wife enough trouble, I would thank you to keep your distance from them while you're here."

Thomas nodded, as his friend wished him to, for it was an easy enough promise to keep. Miss Mystery—Miss Baxter, it seems—was an odd puzzle, but not worth the trouble. No matter how intriguing or entertaining she was. And as Ashbrook led him away, it wasn't Miss Baxter or the mystery surrounding her family that occupied his attention. Her words played through his mind, poking and prodding him with each recounting.

False. Fake.

Never had anyone spoken to him in such a manner, but with each attempt to defend himself from such aspersions, Thomas found himself less and less able to combat them.

People noted her hurried escape. Of course, they did. The stares and whispers spurred Charity's feet faster as she fetched her cloak and hurried into the night. Thankfully, her body moved on instinct, drawing her along without thought, for her mind was entirely consumed. Rubbing at her forehead, Charity hurried along the snowy streets, but she could not outrun her conscience. It nipped at her heels, making her move faster as though the distance between her and the assembly rooms would free her from the past nine years. Or her life.

Charity paused at that, her face raising to the sky. No clouds marred the black above, while the stars swirled through the inky darkness, the tiny pinpricks of light covering every inch. Despite the nip in the air, she felt like casting off her cloak; her skin burned and her heart boiled as her mind teemed with thoughts of the past, unchangeable and immovable, and what she longed for, sitting just out of reach.

Dancing slippers were not made for standing in the snow and ice, and only when her toes were well and truly frozen did she move from that spot, her steps plodding slowly home. Her toes stung from the cold, and Charity embraced it, reveling in each prick of pain as though that might absolve her of every hateful word she'd ever said, every time her temper got the better of her, and every cruel thing she'd done.

What was one to do when they despised their life? Change seemed such a simple thing. Habits were difficult to break, but one simply needed to apply oneself, and with time, the new behavior became familiar and that horrid flaw faded into memory. But how does one do so when the world was determined to hold them in place, not accepting the new version of oneself and forever reminding oneself of the monster she once had been?

Was Bristow blind to her attempts? Or did she not deserve redemption after so many years of following in Mama's miserable footsteps?

Charity had no answers—only recriminations. What did it matter if the Lieutenant was mocking her? Did she deserve any better? How many young ladies had she tormented in such a fashion in her younger years? It was fitting that the world wouldn't let her change, trapping her amongst the Baxters' ranks yet not truly belonging to them.

Those thoughts haunted her as she entered her family's townhouse and took the stairs to her bedchamber; the last of her strength ebbed as she reached the door, just managing to shuffle in and sink to the window seat on the far end of the room.

"Happy Christmas, Charity," she whispered as she rested her forehead against the icy pane.

Chapter 4

In theory, naming a child after a virtue seemed a wise idea, as though it imbued the babe with a hearty dose of the characteristic their parents most wished them to embody. But in reality, it doomed the wee one, burdening them with grand expectations. Especially when it involved such a grand attribute.

Charity. Not just the giving of alms, but the purest, truest, and most unselfish love there was. What lady could live up to such goodness? Granted, Mama and Papa had likely chosen the moniker because it was fashionable or sounded appealing, but Charity Baxter felt the weight of her given name.

However, that old battle had not been the cause of the last two restless nights. Oh, no. Falling short of that impossible standard was one matter altogether, but on Christmas Eve, Charity had gone beyond mere mortal weakness. Without thought, she'd mocked not only the notion of hospitality and generosity to strangers but disrespected the sacredness of the day they celebrated. Charity, indeed.

Time hadn't lessened the growing guilt, for she couldn't banish the Lieutenant from her mind. And each recounting only added to the tightness in her chest and the sour twist of her stomach. Something needed to be done if she wished to have any peace. Whatever anyone else thought of her, Charity would be better than she had been.

And that meant an apology.

Pulling her cloak closer, Charity shifted the basket in her hands as she tromped down the snowy lane that led away from Bristow proper and into the countryside. Clouds of vapor left her lips as she recited what she might say to the Lieutenant, rehearsing yet again the speech she'd prepared. It was far easier to focus on the words themselves than her destination.

The scent of ginger, nutmeg, and cloves wafted up from the basket, and she prayed (not for the first time) that the Lieutenant liked fruitcake. Humble pie was a bitter dish and best served with a side of something sweet. Many a sour mood could be cured with a bit of sugar and fat baked together.

Nature was silent in the winter months, leaving the crisp air empty except for the sound of her boots crunching against the snowy lane. Though Charity missed the birdsong, there was something uniquely beautiful about a winter day when the sun shone bright and the air still. It was strangely comforting. Not that she deserved it.

Letting out a heavy puff of air, which snaked through the chill air, Charity winced as the memories of two nights ago played through her mind again. Casting her thoughts beyond that moment, she combed through the years and wondered if she was any better than before. She certainly liked to think she had improved. Incrementally, at least. Though the Lieutenant likely thought her as horrid as all the rest.

As the road turned and a new lane sprouted out, Charity felt as though she was walking to the hangman's noose. Forcing her feet forward, she followed it along while a prayer rang through her heart—please let the Ashbrooks be gone. Charity required the Lieutenant present to hear her apology, but they needn't be.

The likelihood of them abandoning their guest in such a fashion was not great, but she couldn't help but hope that she'd be free to speak with the gentleman without an audience. Especially them. Perhaps providence would smile upon her and the Ashbrooks would be at Avebury Park, visiting the Kingsleys; as Mr. Ashbrook and his wife lived in the estate's dower house, Charity suspected the brother and sister spent many afternoons together.

Gladwell House was nestled some distance away from the main estate (thank the heavens), allowing Charity the ability to avoid glimpsing the Kingsleys at the very least. The snow gathered on its eves and timbers, making the Tudor cottage all the quainter for it, though with Charity's insides squirming about, it was impossible to admire its picturesque quality.

The manservant who answered had the good sense not to show any shock, but Charity felt the curiosity brew in his mind as he admitted her, and with one sentence, he crushed the last of her hope.

"The family is in the parlor," he said, guiding her into the house. It ought not to surprise Charity that her luck was sour, for she had little experience with the good kind. Yet that didn't stop her heart from sinking as she marched after the manservant.

This was not about the Ashbrooks. They did not matter. She was here to apologize to the Lieutenant. That was all.

The family was, indeed, precisely where the manservant had said. Mrs. Ashbrook's son from her first marriage (Felix? Phillip? Charity could not recall the child's name) sat to one side of the room with his soldiers arrayed around him, his stepfather standing beside him with toys positioned around where the fellow had been seated on the floor. Mrs. Ashbrook stood beside him, ready to welcome their intruder, her expression far more impassive than her husband's, who watched Charity with narrowed eyes.

And there stood the Lieutenant, his seat positioned just behind the boy, as though ready to give the child instructions on how to crush Mr. Ashbrook's forces. The Lieutenant was the only one who looked interested in seeing her, though the twist of his lips hinted that it was more amusement and curiosity than true pleasure. Not that it mattered; Charity was not here for a coze.

"Miss Baxter, do come in," said Mrs. Ashbrook, motioning for the seat, though the stilted tone and stiff movements testified that those were not the words the lady wished to say.

"No need," replied Charity with a shake of her head. Gathering her courage and putting on her blinders, she ignored the others and stepped forward, lifting the basket to the Lieutenant. Her dismissal of the others was uncharitable, but she was reaching the limit of her reserves.

Charity nodded for him to take the basket, and forcing in a deep breath, she turned her thoughts away from him and the others in the room. This wasn't about them. Not truly. She doubted the Lieutenant felt even a twinge of hurt from her words, but her guilt was lashed to her back, unwilling to lighten her burden until she acknowledged what she'd done. They say a conscience was a gift to help one make the right decisions, but at present Charity rather wished she'd never grown one. Mama never seemed bothered.

Dropping her gaze so she could focus on that which was important, Charity let out the words she'd practiced, "I owe you an apology. I spoke harshly to you at the Thompsons' Christmas Eve party, and that was unkind of me. I was out of sorts and made you the focus of my temper, which is entirely unfair of me. Especially as you are a guest in our town, Lieutenant..."

Charity couldn't stop the wince from flashing across her face, but she tucked it away, hoping they hadn't noticed. But that awful Lieutenant smirked at her, his dimples on full display as he studied her.

"Would you like an introduction?" he asked with a spark of mischief in his eyes.

That wretch! Here she was, attempting to do the proper thing—no, the charitable thing—and he was mocking her once again.

Fire flashed in Miss Baxter's gaze, and Thomas struggled not to laugh. He ought to let her say her peace and leave, but he couldn't help but twit her; the lady stood there with all the regality of Anne Boleyn, unwilling to lose her dignity even with the executioner's ax swinging above her. There was something so dramatic about it all, and Thomas couldn't help but find the humor in it, even as Miss Baxter kept waving the basket before him.

It smelled heavenly.

The pair stood there in silence as she fumed, and Thomas finally slanted a gaze at his friend, wondering if the chap was ever going to give the introduction. But Ashbrook merely stared at the lady, his brows twisted together. The fellow's wife seemed no more inclined to speak, while the lad ignored them all and continued to battle it out with his soldiers.

"Ashbrook," murmured Thomas, drawing the fellow's gaze. With a nod towards Miss Baxter, he raised his brows, snapping Ashbrook out of his stupor.

"Miss Charity Baxter, might I introduce Lieutenant Thomas Callaghan." Though Ashbrook spoke the proper words, his tone lacked any inflection, making it sound like he was rattling off instructions to a cabin boy who ought to know better.

However, Thomas was more interested in Miss Baxter's given name. He tried to fight it—he truly did—but he couldn't help the snicker that sprang forth. Though he stifled it, Miss Baxter's eyes narrowed on him.

"I apologize, Miss Baxter," he said. "I did not mean—"

"Yes, you did, Lieutenant Callaghan. For laughing at me is precisely what you enjoy doing best," she said with a huff. "But that is neither here nor there. I am well aware of the hypocrisy of my given name, but as my parents did not consult me when they chose it, I can only accept that it is mine and make the best of it."

With another sigh (which seemed to be the lady's most common form of communication), she straightened her shoulders. "I am here to offer my apology and a peace offering. I hope

I did not offend you."

For all that Miss Baxter affected a grumbly demeanor as she spoke those words, Thomas sensed an earnestness to them. She was so determined to play the martyr, laying her pride on the altar, though without the usual pomp and self-aggrandizing that those types of people usually employed in such circumstances. No, her words were curt and straightforward and entirely honest, offering up what she thought was right, and Thomas suspected it mattered little whether or not he accepted. Miss Baxter was here to speak her peace.

Good for her.

Miss Baxter shoved the basket at him, and Thomas finally took it from her, peeling back the bit of linen as the scent of spices hit him.

"I wanted to bring something finer, but I fear most of our sweets were given away in our Christmas boxes today," she said.

The treat was little more than raisins and currants fused together with a bit of spice cake, but it had been some time since Thomas had enjoyed a proper fruitcake, and with it still warm, it was a fine offering indeed.

"My thanks, Miss Baxter," he said with a smile. "I would be hard-pressed to nurse a grudge with such an apology as this. Sugar and fat baked together in such a manner can cure every ill."

Her brows rose at that, and Miss Baxter's eyes widened, though Thomas couldn't say what was so shocking about that statement.

"I agree," she murmured.

Holding the basket close, Thomas leaned in and lowered his voice. "Does this mean we are to be the best of friends now?"

Miss Baxter's brows pulled into another hard scowl, and she huffed, that little puff of air full of such righteous indignation as though his statement was an affront to decent people everywhere. Was there any wonder he found such delight in twitting her? If Miss Baxter wished him to stop, she should make herself a far less amusing target.

"I have no desire to be your friend, Lieutenant. I do not care for your behavior nor wish to be party to it, but I am ashamed of my own and wished to apologize for it. That is all."

And with that Miss Baxter bobbed a curtsy and spun on her heels.

"Would you join us for a few minutes?" he asked. "Warm yourself a little before you tromp off back home?"

Miss Baxter didn't pause in her retreat, merely calling over her shoulder, "No, thank you."

Mrs. Ashbrook followed on her heels, accompanying her to the front door, and a moment later it shut, and the whirlwind was gone.

Thomas barked out a laugh and flopped onto the seat beside Phillip, resting the basket on his lap as he broke off a bit of the cake and offered it to the lad before taking a healthy chunk for himself. He offered the basket to Ashbrook, but he waved it away. His friend returned to his place on the floor beside his stepson, though his gaze remained on Thomas.

"Must you flirt with Miss Baxter?" he finally asked.

"That was more teasing than flirtatious," replied Thomas, popping another bit of cake in his mouth. The cinnamon and ginger warmed his tongue, and the sweetness of the dried fruit blended with the spices into absolute perfection. "I'd forgotten how much I love fruitcake. Maybe I ought to rile Miss Baxter up more and see if she'll bring me a whole cartful in apology."

"We can make you as much as you'd like."

That earned Ashbrook a smile, as Thomas took another bite. "Ah, but it is all the tastier when delivered by a woman in a temper."

Ashbrook scoffed. "Then you are a fool. I'd rather face down a fleet of French frigates than my wife in a temper. And if you think any of the Baxters are entertaining, you are a fool of the highest order."

Thomas waved it away. Silence fell, and he occupied himself with his fruitcake, wondering if he ought to save half for later or simply enjoy his bounty all at once. For all his jesting about irritating Miss Baxter further, there was an element of truth to it; no doubt, their paths would cross again, and he might just earn himself more in the future.

And thinking about that was far more entertaining than waiting for Ashbrook to speak. Thomas may play the fool, but he recognized the signs of someone gathering their courage, and he guessed what was coming next.

"It is good to see you showing an interest in a lady, Thomas, even if she is a terrible choice."

And there it was.

Thomas laughed. "Intrigued and irritated, certainly, but I am not 'interested' in Charity Baxter. Though you've been an old married man for over a year, I hardly think that long enough to have forgotten how amusing—and harmless—flirting is."

"I've been married nearly two years, thank you very much," replied Ashbrook. "But—"

"It's nothing, Ashbrook," said Thomas with a laugh. "I have lasses pining for me in every port. How else is a sailor to entertain himself ashore? It's naught but a bit of fun. That is all."

Ashbrook frowned, his brow furrowing but not in the amusing manner of Miss Baxter's. No, it was like a grumpy bear contemplating whether or not to swat at you. Miss Baxter, on the other hand, was like a honey badger. Feisty creatures, they were. Thomas had stumbled across one during a trip ashore at the Cape. The small, black and white creatures looked harmless enough, but they possessed such a temper and ferocity that they defeated creatures far larger than they. Thomas had a few scars on his calf to prove just how vicious they could be.

Perhaps Thomas had a wicked streak, but Miss Baxter's grumpiness was far more intriguing than Ashbrook's, even if the latter's was less harmful to Thomas's health.

"I know you've had a rough go of it the last few years," said Ashbrook.

Leveling a hard look at his friend, which was only half-feigned, Thomas shook his head. "There is no need to bring that up."

"Miss Berry—"

"Isn't important anymore, Ashbrook. I count myself a lucky man for having freed myself of such a fickle lady." His insides squirmed, but Thomas shoved it aside. He was better off without that woman in his life. No truer words were ever spoken. Then setting aside the basket, Thomas turned a speculative look at his friend. "I would much rather discuss the reason why you and your family seem so set against the Baxters."

Ashbrook straightened. "Is the reason not clear enough? They are awful people."

"Miss Baxter just delivered a sincere apology with a peace offering to boot. That hardly seems fitting for an 'awful person.'"

"From the moment my sister arrived in Bristow as Mrs. Simon Kingsley, that family has done everything they can to undermine her standing amongst the community and even within her marriage," said Ashbrook with a frown. "And that animosity has been applied to myself and my wife now that we've settled here. Though it bothers me not one bit, Tabby has been wounded by their vicious tongues more than once. They are poisonous, the lot of them."

Turning his gaze to Phillip's soldiers, Ashbrook shifted the figures about. "I do not know what Miss Baxter's game is, but I assure you, it will not end well for you."

Chapter 5

With her back straight, Charity surveyed the gathering, her eyes drifting over the revelers. As the evening was still early, many availed themselves of conversations rather than the myriad of entertainments the Drakes provided. In the salon, gentlemen and ladies gathered around card tables, which would likely see a fortune pass across their wooden surfaces before the night was over.

A pantomime occupied the drawing room with rows of chairs arcing out from the makeshift stage, though the poor actors were performing for an apathetic audience. As the night wore on and the punch flowed, that would change; for now, the entertainers did their level best to keep up their spirits.

Then parlor games in the parlor, of course. Charity didn't think the name denoted the required space in which they ought to be performed, but that was neither here nor there. Groups gathered in different corners with their forfeit keepers organizing them into contests that were bound to lead to laughter and ample amounts of silliness—with or without the punch's aid.

Charity paused at the threshold of the dining room, the scent of the pies, tartlets, biscuits, and cakes calling to her. If not for the knot in her stomach, she would delve into the feast.

Trays and dishes lay thick on the table until hardly an inch of the tablecloth could be seen, begging for her to taste them. But her nerves were wound too tightly for such things.

Tonight would be different. It would be. New Year's Day marked a new beginning, after all. This was the perfect opportunity to begin again. To be this better Charity Baxter. It may take time for others to recognize and accept this improved version, but she only needed to be patient. They would come around.

Eventually.

Despite how firmly she clung to that belief, Charity's insides fluttered like vengeful butterflies, and she drifted past the dining room to continue her rounds through the Drakes' home. Pausing in each room, Charity surveyed the crowd before moving on, searching for heaven knows what, though her feet would not allow her to rest.

"Charity, there you are. Where have you been hiding? I've been looking for you everywhere," said Mama, and then taking her daughter by the arm, she dragged Charity back to the dining room. "There is a gentleman who is quite keen to make your acquaintance. He is the cousin of Mr. Smollet and is visiting for a few days before journeying to the Continent. He is quite the traveler."

Charity couldn't help but notice her mother's vice-like grip on her arm, and instinct had her dragging her feet, though it did no good.

"Mr. Honeyfield," said Mama as they approached, and the gentleman turned to face them. Charity had the good sense not to gape, but her muscles tensed as she stared at a man who had passed his prime long before she'd been born.

"Miss Baxter," he said, bowing low over her hand, which she might've thought grand and mannerly, if it hadn't had the unfortunate effect of causing his head to swing close to hers, assailing her with a strong waft of something fetid. Was the gentleman not acquainted with soap or cologne?

When he straightened, Mr. Honeyfield gripped his lapels

and posed as though waiting for her to paint his portrait. His features and physique were fine for a man of his years, and despite the graying hairs and wrinkles, it was clear he'd been quite handsome in his youth, but that cocky posture and glint in his eye detracted from any appeal he may have possessed once upon a time.

"I spied you when I arrived and just had to seek an introduction." His gaze drifted the length of her figure, not bothering to hide his assessment, and Charity's hand lifted to her neckline, covering the bare expanse as she glanced at the people around her, though she knew no rescue was forthcoming.

"And she is pleased to make your acquaintance, Mr. Honeyfield," said Mama.

Charity's eyes darted to her mother and back to the gentleman as he stepped forward to offer up his arm. Not giving her daughter any choice in the matter, Mama forced her forward, and Charity tried to hold onto her smile as Mr. Honeyfield promenaded her about the house, following a similar route to her previous one.

His stench was even worse up close. One's visage and figure were beyond one's control. A gentleman could not make himself broad-chested with dark locks and piercing blue eyes any more than a lady weave her locks into gold or make her complexion alabaster perfection. However, one's hygiene was quite easily regulated, and Mr. Honeyfield's negligence made Charity gag.

There was a putrid quality to the scent that made Charity fear for her health. Surely, the vapors emanating from his person were harmful. It made her wish she were armed like those in medieval times, who used posies of lavender to ward off the foul air that carried the Black Death. Breathing through her mouth, she refused to allow even the slightest breath of air into her poor, abused olfactory system.

"It is a shame they do not have dancing tonight," he said, leaning in close.

Dear heavens! His breath was even worse, and Charity tried to inch away, but Mr. Honeyfield's arm anchored her to him.

Had he never heard of tooth powder?

"I do love a good turn about the floor with a maiden," he said with a wink and a tone that turned those innocent words into something decidedly wicked as he raised his free hand to rest at the small of her back, his fingers rubbing circles in her flesh. Mr. Honeyfield may not care for bathing, but Charity certainly felt as though she needed one.

Charity glanced at her mama from over her shoulder, but there was no aid to be found there; the lady merely smiled as though he was the grandest of beaus and not some decaying roué. Then Mr. Honeyfield leaned closer and took in a deep breath, letting it out in a low hum—almost a groan—that carried only to her ears. The feel of his breath brushing against her ear had her insides roiling and her skin crawling.

"Punch!" Charity halted and gave him a bright smile. "I am in desperate need of something to drink, Mr. Honeyfield."

He turned to drag her there, but she dug in her heels and patted his arm. "Would you fetch it for me, please?"

Dropping her arm, he swept into another low bow, sending out another wave of stench, and Charity carefully raised a finger to press it to her nostrils, though that did little good to protect the poor appendage.

Mr. Honeyfield turned on his heels, and Mama immediately took his place at Charity's side. "Isn't he perfect, my dear? I overheard him telling Mr. Smollet that he wishes to settle and wants a good wife who needn't be in the first blushes of youth but still able to get him an heir."

Charity's gaze jerked around to see if anyone had overheard them, but no one paid them any mind. When her eyes met Mama's again, the lady was fairly beaming.

"It would be an answer to our prayers."

"Whose prayers?" replied Charity with a raise of her brows.

Mama huffed. "Do not be coy, my dear. It does no good to pretend."

Leaning closer, her brows furrowed as her voice lowered,

"Your prospects have vanished, and you cannot expect to remain in our household forever. Mr. Honeyfield has a comfortable estate and income. You could do far worse."

"Than marry an old, diseased rake? I challenge you to find a worse match."

With a sigh, Mama shook her head. "I have tried my best, but there is nothing I can do. We haven't the luxury to be choosy at this juncture. Those dreadful Kingsleys had ruined all your prospects, so you must seize whatever opportunity comes your way."

The world closed in on her as though invisible walls pressed tight, squeezing her until Charity couldn't move. Couldn't breathe. She was trapped in an invisible box with no way to free herself.

The Kingsleys. Why did everything lead back to them? It felt as though the whole of her life had been dictated by Simon Kingsley, set in place by that one decision he'd made nine years ago.

Charity gagged at the thought of Mr. Honeyfield's lips on hers, his hands touching her, submitting to his whims and pleasures. Fighting for breath, she tried to see some good in the situation, but she could not imagine any quality or blessing he possessed that could overcome his lasciviousness, his boorishness, and all the rest; his hygiene may be the most obvious mark against him, but it was by no means the strongest.

But there was no escaping it, was there? The Kingsley had trapped her in this prison, and the time of reckoning had come. With Mama and Papa forcing the issue, what defense could she mount?

Dropping her gaze, Charity squeezed her eyes shut, struggling to make her lungs work.

Nudging up her chin, Mama patted her daughter's cheek. "Make the best of it."

The strength ebbed from her, and Charity nodded, for what else was there to do?

Chapter 6

Accepting the Drakes' invitation had been a mistake. Of course, Thomas was known to make plenty of those, but this one seemed monumentally daft. Ashbrook and his pretty wife were enjoying a quiet evening at home with Phillip, and instead, Thomas Callaghan (fool that he was) wandered the Drakes' rooms, searching for a diversion. The card games were not challenging enough to tempt him, the parlor games were hardly entertaining when amongst strangers, and Thomas was in no mood for the pantomimes, humorous though they were in other circumstances.

He ought to have followed Ashbrook's example and remained at Gladwell House. To sit about, watching whilst his friend lavished his wife with affection.

Thomas frowned, his lip curling. The imposing Captain Graham Ashbrook spent his time mooning about like a lovesick puppy. Thomas sighed. Perhaps his friend wasn't as bad as all that, but every look the pair shared seemed steeped in sentiments far too private for witnesses. Surely, two years was long enough that the boiling heat of new love had calmed to a simmer. Not that Thomas's would have.

Images snuck into his thoughts, ones so familiar that they

were like old friends settling in for a comfortable coze. Those fantasies had kept him company during long months when *she* had been far from him, out of reach except in his dreams.

Scowling at himself, Thomas shook free of those thoughts. This was precisely why he was at the Drakes.

His gaze drifted through the crowds, searching for any distraction—and spied a certain brunette beauty standing to one side. Thomas smiled, his feet pointing him in that direction, for nothing the Drakes provided would be more amusing than Miss Baxter. Thomas covered a chuckle as he drew up beside her, picturing the way her eyes would narrow at the sight of him.

"Good evening, Miss Baxter," he said, sweeping into a low bow. Thomas straightened and turned his most charming of smiles on her, but it faltered when his gaze met hers. Yes, there was that tensing of her muscles and furrow of her brow he'd anticipated, but her eyes held no wariness or irritation. No fury. Those hazel depths were dim, as though that light within had been snuffed out.

"Lieutenant Callaghan, I didn't realize you were joining us tonight." No huff of annoyance. No stiffening of her spine. Miss Baxter spoke with all the calm politeness expected, yet it had Thomas fighting back a frown. "Have you met Mr. Honeyfield?"

The lady motioned to the gentleman opposite her, and Thomas's brows shot upward at the sight of the wretched pile of bones. The gentlemen exchanged the correct greetings, but Thomas's gaze narrowed as Mr. Honeyfield drew up next to Miss Baxter, slipping her arm through his in a manner that made it clear to even the most oblivious of observers that he viewed the lady as his.

No wonder Miss Baxter was out of sorts. Though they had never met before, Thomas knew Mr. Honeyfield's type. Such men spent their lives steeped in debauchery, choosing to settle down only once they were too plague-ridden and infirm to attract anyone of sense; then they purchased themselves a bride in order to flood the world with their heirs (or rather, their *le-*

gitimate heirs) and secure themselves a nursemaid in their dotage.

"Mr. Honeyfield was telling me of his hunting dogs," said Miss Baxter with all the animation of a corpse.

Thomas scoffed. "Surely, there are far more entertaining subjects."

"You do not hunt, sir?" asked Mr. Honeyfield with the sort of shock usually reserved for the untimely passing of a loved one.

"As I am a creature of the sea, I hardly have the opportunity," replied Thomas, waving a hand down his front to highlight his naval uniform.

"Egads, that is rum business," said Mr. Honeyfield. "I cannot imagine my life without dogs. They are such intelligent creatures. Surely, even a ship would be fare with a dog aboard."

"Perhaps, but I doubt the animal would thank us if we attempted it," said Thomas, turning a laughing look at Miss Baxter, but the lady stood there, her eyes focused on nothing with her arm stiffly threaded through Mr. Honeyfield's.

"I cannot imagine a life without them," continued Mr. Honeyfield. "During hunting season, I spend more time atop a horse than I do with my feet on the ground—"

"As much as I'd love to hear you recount all the virtues of hunting dogs, I fear I promised Miss Baxter a few rounds of parlor games," said Thomas, feeling not the slightest bit guilty for the lie. For all that honesty was a good thing, there were moments when fibs were not only permissible but necessary.

Miss Baxter finally met his gaze fully, a stirring of life returning to those hazel depths.

Mr. Honeyfield frowned. "That may be, Lieutenant—"

But before the bounder could form any proper protest, Thomas snatched her from his hold and led her away.

"I will return her in a few minutes," called Thomas from over his shoulder. Yet another lie of the necessary variety

He didn't slow their rapid retreat until they reached the parlor, but he didn't lead her into the thick of things; instead, he guided her along the edge of the room, and they strolled in silence for several long moments before Thomas finally slanted a look in her direction.

"You may thank me at any time."

Miss Baxter's brows pinched together. "For what?"

"Rescuing you," he replied with a cocky smile that would've had any other lady tittering. The one at his side frowned.

"It is merely a stay of execution," she murmured, the life draining from her gaze once more.

"Then perhaps I'll have to follow you around and fend off Mr. Honeyfield." Thomas laughed, but it earned him none in return.

"It will do no good. The fellow and my parents are keen on the match, and I am expected to simply smile and agree." There was no mistaking the bitterness in her tone, and considering what she was saying, Thomas thought Miss Baxter deserved to feel so.

"All the more reason you require a knight to sweep in and rescue you from that ogre."

Miss Baxter pulled him to a stop, her expression tightening as she glared at him. "Must you make light of everything?"

"The world is better with a bit of frivolity. We all need to laugh more often."

"What do you know of my needs? After a few shallow conversations, are you an expert on them?"

"Shallow conversations?" Thomas blinked. "I thought them entertaining."

With a sigh, Miss Baxter turned away. "If you do not wish to speak of anything substantive, then go amuse yourself by twitting someone else. I am done being the victim of your mockery."

"Victim?" Thomas straightened.

"I am not entertained by your teasing, yet you persist in following me about, ridiculing me at every turn. How else would you describe me but as a 'victim' of your humor?"

Straightening, Thomas studied the lady as she marched

away. No one paid them any heed, but he felt as though she had stripped him bare in front of the group, leaving him on display for all to gape and stare. Miss Baxter's accusation rang in his thoughts, and before he knew what they were up to, his feet were chasing after her.

With her arms crossed, she tucked herself into a corner, and when he approached, her eyes narrowed. "If you are simply going to laugh away my thoughts and feelings, I would rather stand here alone."

Thomas winced. "Then let me be honest and tell you that hearing my company is worse than being alone at a party is sobering."

"You could do with a dose of sobriety. Not everything is a jest."

"So I see," he replied with a nod. "I do not have any fruitcake on hand, but may I apologize for my behavior? I did not mean to cause you pain. I only wished to make you smile."

Her gaze lowered to the floor. "I fear I am out of sorts."

"Are you ever in sorts?" The jest flew from his lips before he had the chance to stop it, but rather than a scowl, it was met with a raise of her brows. Miss Baxter studied him, her eyes holding such bone-deep sorrow that Thomas felt it in his own heart.

"I'm afraid to admit that the answer is 'no.'" Letting out a low sigh, she pressed a hand to her head before giving it a shake. "I suppose I owe you an apology again—"

"Not at all. If I am going to amuse myself by poking badgers, I ought to expect a bite from time to time," he said, recalling the previous image he'd conjured of her. Yes, a honey badger was a perfect likeness for this lady, and perhaps he had self-destructive nature, but Thomas couldn't help but admire her for that feistiness.

"Well, I apologize all the same," she said with an upturn of her lips that hardly qualified as a smile. "I fear I am just so very tired."

Habit supplied a flippant response about needing a better

bed, but Thomas waved it aside. "And what has you 'so very tired?'"

Miss Baxter huffed, a sound full of self-deprecation and bitterness that his heart twinged for the poor creature. Doubly so when her gaze met his, the truth of her words stepped in those hazel depths as she said, "Everything."

Another snappy retort came to mind, and Thomas paused. Truly, was that his instinctual response to every heavy subject? Frowning at himself, he tucked that quandary away.

"Perhaps this New Year might bring about some changes to your life," he replied. That earned him a sigh, and she turned away, but he held up his hands in surrender. "I am not jesting, Miss Baxter. I truly mean it. We never know what the future might bring."

"That may be true for those who sail off to new horizons, but for nearly a decade, my life has remained precisely as it is—no matter what I do to alter its course. I hardly think that this year will be any different."

"But consider just how much of the New Year celebrations are steeped in divining what is to come. The air is filled with the hope of new things. Might not you borrow a dash of that good cheer for yourself?"

"That is tempting, Lieutenant Callaghan," she replied with a hesitant smile. "What is your tried-and-tested source of New Year divination?"

Tucking his hands behind him, Thomas's thoughts were cast back to days he hadn't considered in a very long time. There were traditions aplenty aboard ships, but as they were created by bored men stuck together in tight quarters, there was nothing suitable to share with a lady—especially one angered by ridiculousness. So, he turned his memories of that time before he'd donned his first naval uniform. His heart grew heavy as memories of his childhood home played through his thoughts, bringing with it a young Thomas who had thought that simple life would be forever his.

Blinking, Thomas straightened and yanked his thoughts

back to where they ought to be. “Have you heard of first-footing?”

Miss Baxter shook her head.

“Ah,” he said with a broad smile. “It is a tradition in the North. Guaranteed accurate.”

“Is that so?” she replied with an arched brow.

“Laugh not, Miss Baxter.” Thomas gave her a winning smile. “It is said that the first person to come into your home on New Year’s Day is a portent of the luck and blessings for the year. It is such a universal fact that families take great care with whom they invite to cross their threshold on that auspicious day.”

Miss Baxter’s brows furrowed together. “So they believe it is a portent, but go about manipulating it so the right person crosses their threshold first?”

“And have them bear gifts to symbolize all the good fortune that is to come,” he said with a nod.

“That seems suspect.”

“But true enough that my father was given all sorts of bribes to visit the neighbors first thing on New Year’s Day.” Then, leaning close, Thomas gave a gentle nod at humor by adding. “Our family was considered steeped in good luck.”

Never mind that the Callaghans had none for themselves, but that never stopped the others from believing the tradition.

“Is that so?” she asked with another arched brow.

“Yes, a dark-haired, handsome man is the pinnacle of good fortune.” Then Thomas winked at her, and though she huffed at that ridiculousness, Miss Baxter’s lips turned up with a hint of humor—however unwilling.

“Dark hair?”

“The darker, the better. Nothing is worse than a fair-haired lady.”

Miss Baxter laughed at that, a sharp, halting thing as she shook her head. “I would have you know that the first person to cross our threshold was likely Mrs. Ellis, who paid a call on my mother early this morning.”

"A lady?"

"Most certainly."

Thomas considered that. "And her hair—"

"Quite fair, Lieutenant Callaghan. Even before it grayed, it was as fair as fair can be."

"Goodness," he said, rocking back on his heels. "That does not bode well. Perhaps she brought some gift to offset her ill fortune."

But Miss Baxter shook her head. "Only poisonous gossip and a sharp tongue."

Sucking in a deep breath, Thomas let it out in a low whistle. "I fear you and your family are doomed."

The young lady gave a true, deep laugh at that, though her hand flew to her mouth as though to hold it in. When Thomas joined in, Miss Baxter let it loose, embracing the ridiculousness of the moment for once.

With a sad shake of her head, she added, "I am a hopeless cause."

"Not at all, Miss Baxter," he said with a gentle smile. "But it might help if you learned to laugh at yourself. Life is full of disappointments, and humor is the only way to manage them."

She straightened and considered him for a long, silent moment. Her eyes held his, and it felt as though she reached right into him. Thomas widened his grin, but that did nothing to deter her study of him. And like before, it felt as though that one glance stripped him bare, peering into the very heart of him. Thomas fought not to squirm beneath the regard, and turning to the group at the far corner, he pointed towards them.

"I adore *All in Suds.* Would you do me the honor of joining me for a round or two?" he said.

But Miss Baxter's gaze narrowed for another long moment before she nodded and took his arm, allowing him to drag her into the fray.

Chapter 7

Gripping Lieutenant Callaghan tightly, Charity followed him along, hardly daring to meet the others' eyes as he inserted them into the circle of people. Though she earned a few narrowed looks, the majority ignored her, which was a better reception than she'd anticipated. Of course, it helped that her companion eased her way in with a few cheeky remarks, which set the group laughing.

This was precisely the sort of gathering that suited a man like Lieutenant Callaghan. His ridiculousness knew no bounds, and each attempt outdid the last until even her harshest critics would gladly welcome her presence if it included his company. They laughed and jeered, goading him to greater heights of silliness. Never seeing behind the smiling mask.

Did no one else recognize it? Charity's brow furrowed as she considered it. But what did she know of the fellow? Hardly a thing. All she had was instinct warning her that those dimples hid something darker. She frowned, and when that drew the attention of the young lady to her right, Charity shifted back into a polite smile, nodding at her; Miss Wilson turned away with a silent huff.

Holding back a sigh, Charity's thoughts returned to Lieutenant Callaghan. Here she sat, attempting to pick apart his motivations and feelings after a few short conversations with him—and not a single one held any significance. She paused in her mental meandering and considered that. Perhaps that was the problem; the Lieutenant avoided any serious subject. Though Charity would swear before a magistrate that it wasn't because he lacked depth; for all that he played the jester, that was something far more intelligent and feeling beneath the frivolous façade.

But such thoughts vanished when the game's conductor rose and stood in the center. With a loud voice, he gave them a dramatic speech, full of feigned sorrow. "Despite this merry time, I know our hearts are quite heavy. You needn't hold in that pain any longer. Please allow yourself to release the breath that so desperately wishes to be freed."

With that, the company all gave heavy sighs. Though Charity had thought her attempt valiant, full of the dismay of a swooning damsel, it paled in comparison to the others—some of whom even went so far as to collapse from their chairs. And in the heart of the chaos was Lieutenant Callaghan, who affected the daintiest sigh in all of existence, waving a hand before his face as though he was about to faint like some wilting violet, and Charity covered her mouth to stifle a laugh.

Turning to the gentleman closest to him, the conductor said, "Ah, me. We are a sorry bunch. Might I trouble you, sir, to tell me your heartache?"

"I cannot find my lost pocket watch."

The conductor nodded with such concern wrinkling his brow that one might think it the most serious of grievances. As the players went round, enumerating their feigned troubles, Charity scoured her thoughts for something that might amuse the gathering. But the conductor arrived at Miss Wilson to her right.

"Mama refuses to serve boiled potatoes at dinner." Acting the part, Miss Wilson added another heavy sigh, as though her heart were ready to break from the lack of boiled potatoes in her life.

Then all the gazes turned to Charity. And she froze. Despite her pariah status, she had participated in parlor games from time to time. Unfortunately, no amount of practice improved her wit and creativity in such circumstances, and now, she was center stage with everyone staring at her, awaiting her contribution to the hilarity.

"I am...ill."

Charity's meager offering was met with silence, and then the conductor nodded, quickly turning to Lieutenant Callaghan to continue the list of ailments.

"I fear, dear ladies and gentlemen, I am suffering greatly," he said with such gravity, his expression a mask of earnest heartache. "Though I mourn deeply for all your woes, I am suffering far more than any of you. For, you see, I am quite desolate. Nay, I am inconsolable. My life is a bleak and wretched thing without any hope of relief."

Lieutenant Callaghan paused, and Charity wondered if the others realized how they leaned closer, like moths drawn to the candle's flame. Only when the silence had drawn out to unbearable levels did he speak.

"I dropped a spot of ink on my shoe." And with that Lieutenant Callaghan wiped away imaginary tears as the rest of the party broke into laughter, and his performance was such a perfect blending of drama and ridiculousness that Charity couldn't help but be swept up in the mirth.

Thankfully as that portion of the game wound to a close, it shifted into its true purpose, of which Charity was quite confident she would triumph. Beginning with a player at random, he repeated his ailment once more and then recited another. The person suffering from the second ailment then repeated the two and added a third, continuing around as the list grew greater and greater.

Charity focused her attention on each player, repeating the list in her thoughts, practicing it as she waited for someone to list her ailment. But Mr. Ingalls stumbled on his recitation, and he groaned in earnest this time as the others all cried out, "Forfeit!" Lifting her list, the forfeit keeper made a mark beside Mr. Ingalls' name, tallying all who owed her punishments by the end of the evening—which were bound to embarrass and elicit laughter in equal measure.

The round began anew, the former list being wiped from their memories as Mr. Ingalls called out his trouble and added another's to it. Again, the recitation grew even longer this time, surpassing the previous round's seven to reach a mighty ten ailments before Mrs. Cavendish stumbled.

"Forfeit!" they cried again, and so the process continued as player after player fell prey to the forfeit keeper.

Lieutenant Callaghan was a favorite, of course, but then he made a grand show of his failures, covering his missteps with jests that poked fun of himself as often as they teased the others. And it was easy for Charity as no one called upon her, though she kept her mind whirling with the lists, forcing herself to remember them again and again. Thankfully. For her ailment was tacked on the end of the longest list they'd managed yet.

All eyes turned to her as Charity took a fortifying breath and began reciting the list, never faltering as she enumerated each heartache before tacking on Mrs. Atwood's. And so, the game continued. Though she was never called on as often as the others, Charity found herself thrown into the mix once the tally grew to difficult lengths. Lieutenant Callaghan smiled at her, his eyes alight with humor as she recited another exceptionally numerous list without stumbling.

With a raise of his brows and mouthed, "Brava."

Charity couldn't help but smile in response.

Mr. Honeyfield notwithstanding, this was the most perfect evening she'd had in a long time. But as she considered that, Charity amended that thought; this may be the best without caveat or exception. Before Mrs. Kingsley arrived in Bristow, Charity's outings had revolved around gossiping and fault-finding, imbuing each gathering with as much joy as Mama found in such things—which was to say none at all. And upon falling from social grace, Charity's evenings had become a drudgery.

Unable to stop herself, she studied Lieutenant Callaghan's profile as he laughed and teased the others. Despite the irritation he often elicited, she couldn't help but feel a warm stirring for this man who had rescued her from Mr. Honeyfield and then lent her his social clout.

Charity's shuddered as she considered how much of her previous standing had been due to fear or awe—never adoration or friendship. Having continued in her mother's footsteps, Charity had been pleased to look down her nose at all the rest, content in her superiority. And only when that power was gone had she understood just how hollow it was. And cruel.

The hard words and judgments. The gossip and maligning. Charity had embraced the power granted to her by her mother's frightening reputation and her own natural beauty, never deigning to empathize with her victims. Until forced into their metaphorical slippers.

The sound of her ailment jerked Charity from her thoughts, and she turned wide eyes to the group. Good heavens. Had she heard the entire inventory? Scouring her thoughts, she recited off the ones she knew with all certainty. Then carefully, she listed one after the other, waiting for cries of "Forfeit!" Charity furrowed her brow as she slogged through the list, praying and hoping it was right.

And then she reached her ailment. Turning to Lieutenant Callaghan with a grin, she tacked on his, and he laughed.

"I don't know if I should even attempt it, for I am certain to fail spectacularly." That earned him a flurry of "forfeits," which he accepted with a nod before suggesting, "How about a round of *I Love My Love with a Letter A*?"

But that was met with groans that rivaled the mock ones they'd given in their current game.

"We need something with more forfeits," said Mr. DeFoe. "Parlor games are best when every player is left with a mountain of them to repay."

Lieutenant Callaghan waggled his brows (how did he manage to do so and look rascally rather than ridiculous at his age?). "You wish for more forfeits, do you? I would think you've had enough of them."

Mr. DeFoe grimaced. "Perhaps I wish to even the playing field with a few rounds of *Toilette*."

That was met with cheers, and the conductor had them quickly arranged as necessary for the game. Soon, the players were up and running around, the play requiring constant shifts between chairs. There were collisions, which set the players laughing. That, in turn, distracted them long enough to misstep, earning them forfeits.

True to Mr. DeFoe's prediction, soon most of the players were laden with more forfeits than anyone ought to have. But with each speedy round, Charity fought through the crowd, finding her way to a safe seat before anyone caught her. Of course, her natural skill was aided by the fact that the group ignored her, allowing her to go undetected through much of the game. Charity smiled as players were flooded with penalties, and she redoubled her efforts, slipping through the chaos to steal chairs from those too slow to catch her.

Throughout it all, she kept a vague tally of the other players. The forfeits flew fast, making it difficult to keep an accurate count, but of one thing she was certain—Charity Baxter had avoided any. Sitting in her pilfered chair, she tried not to preen, but she couldn't keep the smile from her lips. There were no scores kept (and by extension no true winners or losers), but the lack of forfeits on her part certainly felt like a clear indication that she was the most skilled player.

Another mad scurry shook the room, and Charity dashed across, refusing to take the easiest of seats. Mr. Talbot and Mr. DeFoe were so busy trying to steal the spot from each other that Charity slipped around them and seized it out from under them. The gentlemen gaped as they realized their quarry was lost, and quickly shoved each other aside to reach the next one over. A laugh took hold of her, burbling out as she covered her mouth and watched the melee.

Soon, the players were all heaving and red-faced, slumping onto their chairs before begging off. Charity frowned, wishing to protest, but the group slowly dispersed.

"My, my, but there are many of you who owe me forfeits," said the Keeper, waving her record for all to see. "Only Miss Baxter is still free of any debts."

Biting on her lips, Charity forced herself not to smile or give any other sign that might be viewed as crowing. Enjoying her victory was one thing but reveling in it was another altogether and hardly the sort of behavior that would enhance her standing. The others glanced at her, and she gave a bright laugh, searching for that which she might say to dispel some of the hard looks leveled at her.

"Good game!" she said, but frost swept through the air as the others turned cold shoulders to her. Rising to her feet, she held back a sigh and refused to allow her heart to sink; this had been entertaining, whatever the rest of the evening brought.

A glass appeared before her, and her gaze followed the hand to Lieutenant Callaghan's face.

"I am parched, Miss Baxter," he said, taking a drink from his own. "That was quite the rousing game."

But Charity stared at the proffered drink for several silent blinks before grabbing the glass. It was a little thing. A kindness, to be certain, but no more than what any gentleman ought to. Yet she couldn't think of another who had done such—especially as he was not officially escorting her tonight. Their paths had crossed for a bit, but that held little significance. It certainly didn't require him to fetch her refreshments.

"There is no shame in earning forfeits," he said, giving her a side glance as they watched the other mingle.

Charity gave him a wry smile. "Says the gentleman who will be spending most of the night fulfilling his."

But Lieutenant Callaghan shrugged. "It is part of the fun and integral to my strategy as most forfeit keepers will forgive them if you amass a ludicrous amount. However, I simply wanted to assure you that you needn't worry about being put on display. Few forfeit keepers are creative enough to make you do anything truly embarrassing. Certainly nothing shocking."

Raising her brows at that, for Charity was well aware that some loved using that position of power to put people on display in some truly audacious manners, she took a sip of her drink. "I am not afraid of being embarrassed."

That was met with a raise of his brows, and Charity dropped her gaze.

"Perhaps I am." Peeking at him, her lips twisted into a half-smile. "However, I avoid forfeits because I cannot bear to lose."

Lieutenant Callaghan broke into a wide grin. "Ah, so Miss Baxter is excessively competitive is she?"

"Not excessively," replied Charity, but that earned her another raise of his brows, and she shifted in place. "Perhaps I work a tad harder than most to win, but it helps that I have a good memory, which is required for so many of them. When games revolve around wit, I lose every time."

"That cannot be true—"

Charity leveled a look at him. "You did hear my ailment during *All in the Suds*, didn't you? I fear I struggle with creativity and humor."

"You simply do not practice it enough," he replied, taking another sip. But their conversation was cut short when another guest called to her companion. Lieutenant Callaghan moved towards them and paused when she did not follow.

"They did not ask for me," she said.

Lieutenant Callaghan waved it away and nodded for her to join them. Charity didn't know if he noticed the tight lips that showed on the ladies' faces when she stepped up beside him, and Charity fought to keep herself from fidgeting at that displeasure. They may not want her, but he did. Surely, that was enough.

Chapter 8

"We were thinking of playing a round of *Aunty's Garden*," said Miss Ingalls, glancing at her companions. "Have you played before?"

"Never heard of it," said Lieutenant Callaghan while Charity shook her head.

Miss Gilbert stepped up beside Miss Ingalls and beamed. "Oh, it is quite delightful! I learned it at my cousins' home this summer. You will adore it." The young lady's gaze touched Charity before turning away, her smile tightening. "And perhaps it might even earn our dear Miss Baxter her first forfeit of the evening."

The challenge in her tone was clear, and Charity straightened her spine. "Perhaps it might."

With a few words of introduction, they gathered the players around, getting them in a circle as Miss Gilbert stood in the center, taking the role of conductor.

"This is a game of memorization and recitation. I will speak a line, and everyone in the circle must repeat it, one after the other. Once everyone has done so, I will add another, and it will be passed along the circle once more. Then I will add a third line and so on. Anyone who makes a mistake will pay a forfeit."

That was met with a few jeers and twits about the various players' ability to avoid that wretched fate, but then Miss Gilbert raised a hand, and they fell silent.

"I have just come from my Aunt Deborah's garden. Bless me! What a fine sight it is for in my aunt's garden there are four corners."

Many stumbled and tripped over the words, missing little ones here and there, but Charity ignored the rest of them, focusing on Miss Gilbert's words, and when it eventually came to her turn, she managed the whole of it without a single stumble. Miss Gilbert's eyes narrowed briefly, though she quickly turned her smile to the next in line. At Lieutenant Callaghan's turn, he hardly got more than a few words in before he stumbled, adding to the frivolity by laughing at himself as vigorously as any of the others.

The next round went much the same with an equally long recitation added to the first. And yet another, each describing the different plants in the corners of the mythical aunt's garden. The words were little more than nonsense strung together in couplets, but in some ways, the unnatural quality made it easier to recall the proper words than if they had been perfectly sensible. Charity continued to navigate it with little trouble, and the sense of displeasure grew among the young ladies, though the gentlemen seemed not to notice the growing unease. Lieutenant Callaghan cheered heartily with each round Charity perfected, though the others' applause grew fainter with each.

When that round finished, Miss Gilbert continued, "In the third corner Jane showed much pride; let your mouth to your neighbor's ear be applied, and quick to his keeping a secret confide."

Charity stiffened as the others all snickered, laughing behind their hands as ladies blushed and demurred while the gentleman shifted in place.

"Go on," said Miss Gilbert. And so the first in the circle gave the recitation, ending it by leaning to the left and whispering a secret into her neighbor's ear. Both listener and speaker chuckled, and the watching crowd added to the mirth, speculating about the secrets shared. But all Charity could focus on was what she ought to say.

Curse games that required wittiness! Such entertainments were hardly entertaining without heavy doses of comedy, and Charity had never excelled at such things. It was a gift, and where Lieutenant Callaghan had been blessed with an abundance, Charity was certain to dampen the frivolity.

Frowning, she scoured her thoughts for something she could say. Charity glanced at her intended secret keeper and wondered what she might say to Miss Ingalls that was amusing enough to draw a laugh but without embarrassing herself. Unfortunately, nothing came to mind.

And then all eyes were on her. Slowly, she recited the lines, managing to correct herself before she stumbled on the words. Then leaning closer, Charity paused, her thoughts flying through all the possibilities. And then she landed on one. It may not be witty or amusing, but it was true and needed to be said.

"Miss Ingalls," she whispered, "I am sorry for having treated you so poorly in the past. I wish I could undo the harm I've caused you and begin again."

The young lady jerked away, her spine stiffening as she stared at Charity. Neither of them noticed as Lieutenant Callaghan went through his recitation (earning him yet another forfeit), and the spell locking them in place was only broken once he leaned in to whisper into Charity's ear.

"After a particularly grueling day and rough night's sleep, I woke the next morning and dressed. I spent several hours prowling the deck of the ship before realizing I'd put my trousers on backward. The entire crew had noticed and said not a word to me."

Charity snapped her gaze to him, caught between the laugh his secret elicited and the remnant discomfort from her own. His brows furrowed as he watched her, but the game continued as she sat back in her chair, studying her hands as they clenched in her lap.

And that was when Miss Gilbert dropped the true motive of the game, announcing with a broad smile, “In the fourth corner are amaranths, gathered together in a crowd. Now, each secret whispered must be told aloud.”

That drew forth laughter from all those who had not anticipated that twist, and quite a few jeers directed at those who had known what was to come. But Charity’s muscles tensed as the players each exposed the secrets shared with them. Most of them were innocuous little things, but Charity could not focus on them or the laughter erupting around her.

Her secret. To lay that truth bare to all these people, many of whom were quite pleased to have witnessed her downfall. But even as Charity considered the door and her chances of escape, peace settled over her. Perhaps this was for the best. She had long ago wished for a new start. Miss Ingalls had not been the only lady in this circle Charity had harmed in her bid for dominance, and they all deserved a similar apology.

The lady in question recited the couplets and slanted a quick look in Charity’s direction before facing the crowd and saying with a wide grin. “Miss Charity is madly in love with Lieutenant Callaghan and hopes to catch his eye before she ends up a sad, lonely spinster. She is determined to steal a kiss before the night is through!”

And oh, how they laughed. The group reveled in the sound, though it lacked the gentle touch of true mirth. It was sharp and biting, and like cackling hyenas, the scavengers fell upon Charity’s wounded dignity, ripping it to shreds. Despite the derision in that sound, she kept her spine straight and her head held high, clinging to her dignity even in the face of social death.

But then her eyes turned to Lieutenant Callaghan, and he was guffawing so hard it was a miracle he kept his seat. Charity flinched at the sight and fought to remain impassive. Any movement might alert the predators that their prey was not dead. But the sound of him snickering and snorting rang out louder than the rest, drowning out the others as it filled her ears and pierced deep into her heart.

Charity felt exposed. Bare. With the last morsel of her pride devoured, she had nothing left to hide behind. The whole of her was laid out for them to see. And mock.

Throat tightening, she jerked to her feet and fled the parlor amidst the sounds of laughter and cries of "Forfeit!"

Sighing to himself, Thomas wandered the Drakes' home, his eyes drifting through the crowds. But there was no sign of the minx in green. Sucking in another deep breath, he let it out in a heavy breath, and a gentleman to his side glanced at the sound. Thomas nodded at the man as though nothing were amiss and continued on his way.

If Miss Baxter was going to run off and sulk about a good-natured jest, then he ought to leave her to it. Could she not find humor in a game? Why was she so determined to be offended by every little thing? It was little wonder why so many shunned her. Life was intolerable if one couldn't laugh at oneself, and Miss Baxter was far too serious for her own good.

Yet even as Thomas convinced himself to leave her to her moping, the memory of her gaze kept him searching. He had expected to see that same puckered look she got when affronted, all brimming with self-righteous anger. Instead, he'd spied pain. Betrayal.

Having scoured the rooms twice, Thomas had to admit defeat. She was not inside the house.

Thomas tucked his jacket tighter around him as he stepped into the Drakes' courtyard. Darkness enveloped him, blinding him to everything except the candlelight streaming through the windows. A step or two into the black, and his eyes adjusted, though there was hardly any light coming from the moon above, and even that tiny sliver was blocked out by the high walls around them.

The courtyard was not a large space. The walkway was barely wide enough for two people to walk abreast; shrubs edged the pavers, winding outward in geometric shapes that had been carefully shaped and cultivated by the gardeners. The white of the frost and snow caught the candlelight in the windows, reflecting it and helping him to navigate around the small space. But no sign of Miss Baxter.

Another sigh, which sent a billowing puff of vapor out into the chill night air, and Thomas turned back to the door. But sound caught his ear, and he turned back, scouring the shadows. His brow furrowed as he stepped closer, finally spying the edge of skirts peeking out from the black.

"Miss Baxter?" No response. Drawing beside her, Thomas took the seat on the bench, wincing as the cold stone bit at his skin.

"A forfeit is not such a wretched thing. Certainly not worth fleeing the game," he said with a hint of humor, but it elicited no response from Miss Baxter. He didn't know why he had attempted it. Her gaze was fixed upward, studying the sky though the stars were nowhere in sight.

"No one believes Miss Ingalls. That is what made it so humorous. Utter nonsense is amusing," he said, leaning over to nudge her. "Though I would be honored if you wished to kiss me."

Miss Baxter stiffened, and Thomas sighed again, adding, "It was only a jest. She didn't mean any harm. Parlor games are only entertaining when everyone embraces the ludicrousness of it."

Just as Thomas was considering how to get the lady back into the house before she caught her death, a quiet voice answered him, the words so thin and listless that he almost thought he'd imagined them.

"Miss Ingalls meant to harm." Miss Baxter's voice wobbled on the last word, and she shuddered, turning away from him as she curled inwards. Her hands flew to her mouth, but they couldn't muffle the sob that broke loose. Her breaths were jagged, broken things, shaking her as she fought against them.

Chapter 9

With wide eyes, Thomas stared at the sobbing lady. Despite having witnessed many outbursts from Miss Baxter, they had been of the fiery sort, all temper and heat. Reaching forward, he patted her on the shoulder, but that did little good, for she was seized by tears, her muffled cries echoing in the silent courtyard.

"I don't know if I should be offended that you are crying over the thought of kissing me—"

Miss Baxter twisted around enough to glare at him, and she struggled to speak; her broken breaths made it impossible, but Thomas understood her meaning well enough. Now was not the time for jests.

Holding his hands up in surrender, he waited until she turned away once more before lowering them, and his right arm draped around her. Miss Baxter's dainty shoulders felt strange beneath his hand, and she remained stiff and distant for several long moments before surrendering to the emotion and drowning herself in tears once more.

Minutes ticked away and slowly, her sobs lessened, though her breaths were still ragged and uneven.

"Are you feeling better?" Thomas asked, not daring to use

even a hint of humor in the question.

"No."

Having no obvious response for such a confession, Thomas remained silent, and the pair of them stared off at the dark garden while Miss Baxter sniffled.

"Have you ever wished you could start your life over and do things differently?" she asked between shuddering breaths.

"I think everyone does from time to time."

But Miss Baxter turned to study him, her brows knitting tight together. "I am not asking about everyone. Have *you* felt that way?"

Her tone was so earnest, her expression so pleading that though Thomas wished to give her a flippant answer, those words fled him. "Yes."

Miss Baxter let out a low breath and nodded, though Thomas didn't know what she meant by it. "Miss Ingalls and the others meant to mock me, and I am sorry to say that I deserve it. I have treated so many of them poorly."

"Why?"

Brushing at her cheeks, Miss Baxter dropped her gaze to her lap. "I wish I could give some better reason than pride and vanity, but the truth is, I was a mean-spirited person who'd been raised to believe it was my right to lord my position over others. I was the center of society, placed there by my mother's machinations and taught to divorce myself from pity or empathy."

Thomas frowned at that. Though Miss Baxter was a curmudgeon at times, he struggled to imagine her as unfeeling. The lady's heart was so alive and strong, the very antithesis of apathetic; while he could well imagine her being snippish, Miss Baxter felt too deeply to be devoid of sentiment.

When she said nothing more, Thomas prodded her. "What changed?"

Miss Baxter let out a bitter huff. Then, as though speaking to herself, she murmured, "Why not? It's not as though you are going to be in town for long."

"There is relative anonymity in confiding with a stranger." Thomas spoke with a light tone, but again, it missed the mark. Thankfully, Miss Baxter seemed not to hear him as she began laying out her troubled past with the Kingsleys.

Thomas struggled to align her tale with the people he'd come to know since his arrival at Bristow, and he couldn't. Though Mr. Simon Kingsley seemed a tad oblivious at times, it was not meanspirited in nature, and Mrs. Mina Kingsley was the dearest sort of woman. Yet, how often did actions have unintended consequences for others? How often did we hurt others without meaning to, leaving them hurt and bitter against us?

Miss Baxter did not look at him as she recounted her history, but Thomas could not turn away from her. His hand on her shoulder rubbed gently against her, drawing her nearer as they nestled together on the bench. The cold nipped at him, but the burning of his heart staved off the majority of it. That sad organ felt a whisper of that pain, the sorrow and loneliness echoing in every pinched expression as she spoke.

"It changed me," she murmured. "I came to see the cruelty of my behavior, but no matter how I try to atone for my sins or start again, I am forever viewed as that antagonist of old. What little respect I garner now is due to fear of my mother's retaliation, though that would presuppose she notices anything beyond her own interests."

Turning her gaze back up to the sky above, Miss Baxter searched the stars as though they might hold the answers.

"I am so tired. No matter what I do, I will always be the pariah. I am forever marked by the sins of my past, unable to find friendship in new circles. Yet Mama's set disgust me. I have no place in this world," she said in a low voice, the words seeping out into the night air. Then meeting his gaze once more, Miss Baxter's eyes plead with him for some answer or understanding. "No matter what I do, they reject me. They laugh. They mock. They revel in my downfall. I know I deserve everything I am receiving, but how much do I have to suffer before my debt is paid?"

Unable to stop himself, Thomas pulled her close and wrapped her in his arms. His words hadn't helped in the past, and he didn't trust himself to give her any guidance. So, he circled her in his arms, holding her tightly as though that might ease away the agony of so many long, lonely years.

"I would be honored to count you among my friends," he said.

Miss Baxter stiffened, pulling away to stare at him.

Holding up his hands in surrender, Thomas couldn't help the light tone that slipped out as he said, "I know you find my behavior abhorrent and have no desire to be my friend—"

"Did I truly say that?" she groaned, lowering her head.

Thomas cracked a smile. "Yes."

"I do apologize—"

"No need," he said with a wave of his hands. "I am not so easily offended, and I have done my level best to irritate you. I cannot moan and complain when I succeed."

Miss Baxter straightened, her brows raising. She was silent for a long moment, and Thomas prayed his attempt at humor did not fall short as it so often did.

"You are very good at pestering me," she said with the barest hint of a smile.

"You are very good at rising to the bait."

His cautious humor earned him a huff that was almost a laugh.

"I suppose I am, but I have learned that when people are laughing, it is at my expense. And I cannot help but wonder why a gentleman who is so jovial and widely accepted, such as yourself, would care to offer friendship to a humorless outcast like me."

Miss Baxter watched him, waiting for a response, and Thomas squirmed beneath it. In all honesty, he could hardly understand it himself. The lady had no endearing qualities, though seeing Miss Baxter in a dander was far more entertaining than the parlor games.

"I know how it feels to be lonely," he said with a shrug.

The lady's brows drew together, her eyes staring at him, but Thomas pretended to study the shrubbery. A faint smile remained plastered on his lips while memories tickled at the back of his thoughts, attempting to steal away his attention.

With her gaze so fixed on him, Thomas didn't trust himself to wallow in the past, for he was certain she'd see all those dark and dreary days stamped on his face. Those experiences had taught him to stand on his own two feet, but that did not give them the right to dominate his present.

When Miss Baxter didn't speak, Thomas shifted in his seat and said, with a forced laugh, "Besides, though you do not mean to be, you are quite amusing at times."

Miss Baxter frowned, though it seemed more pensive than perturbed. She opened her mouth to speak, and Thomas held his breath, his eyes drifting about the courtyard, though there was little to see in the darkness.

Footsteps broke the silence, cutting off Miss Baxter's words as a lady called from the darkness, "There you are, Charity."

Thank the heavens for Mrs. Baxter. Thomas was certain no one else had ever thought such a thing about her before, but he let out a breath and shot to his feet with a smile.

Standing before her daughter, the lady folded her hands together and frowned. "Why have you abandoned Mr. Honeyfield? He is eager for your company."

"I needed some air, Mama," replied Miss Baxter, smoothing her skirts.

"Enough of that, you cannot waste an opportunity..." But it was as though Mrs. Baxter only just then realized Thomas was standing beside her daughter. A single brow arched as her gaze swept over him. "You must be the Ashbrooks' guest."

With a quick bow, he said, "Lieutenant Thomas Callaghan, madam. Mr. Ashbrook is an old friend of mine. We sailed together for several years."

Mrs. Baxter huffed. "So, I've heard. But I wouldn't broadcast your connection if I were you. That family is not all good and proper—"

"Mama," chided Miss Baxter, though her mother hardly paused as she continued, her tone entirely too smug while her imperious brow arched ever higher.

"I do not know if you were aware of it, but Mrs. Ashbrook—Mrs. Russell then—was his housekeeper, and I shan't sully your ears with all the rumors I heard about what was happening under Mr. Ashbrook's roof. To say nothing of the fact that she was married to another man when they met, and she married again quickly after his mysterious passing. Quite suspicious, if you ask me—"

"I didn't ask you," said Thomas with a narrowed look and a tone that had Mrs. Baxter huffing.

"I only meant to inform you so that you are not sullied by association."

Thomas scoffed. "I know precisely what you meant to do, Mrs. Baxter."

Turning her attention back to her daughter, Mrs. Baxter seized her by the arm. "Come now, Charity. Do not waste your time here when there is a far more important gentleman wishing for your time."

Then with a haughty lift of her nose that mirrored the expression her daughter often employed, Mrs. Baxter dragged her daughter away. Miss Baxter didn't fight her, but she did cast a look over her shoulder, her gaze full of apologies.

Chapter 10

With the curtains pulled tight against the afternoon sun, Charity's bedchamber was shrouded in darkness. Tiny slivers of light snuck around the heavy fabric, giving just enough light for her to see the edge of the canopy draped above her. Rubbing at her temples, she tried to relieve the pressure of her megrim, but it was a useless endeavor. Little sleep meant her head ached, which kept her from sleeping. It was a cycle of torment.

But it was not the pulsing pain that kept her mind too active to slip off into slumber.

Never was there a greater fool than Charity Baxter. She felt like cringing every time she thought of the Drakes' party. And while a lady with far more intelligence might be fixated on the trouble with Mr. Honeyfield, it was Lieutenant Callaghan who occupied the whole of her attention. For all that her stomach churned every time she recalled Mr. Honeyfield's leering looks and the feel of his hand at the small of her back, it was her interlude with Lieutenant Callaghan that had her burying her head beneath her pillows.

Had she truly sobbed like a child in front of him? Whining and moaning about her lot? Burying her face, Charity closed her eyes, but it couldn't stop her thoughts from playing that scene again and again. Hearing every word she'd uttered. Seeing that look of pity on his face.

But then came the phantom feel of his fingers against her shoulder. Those kind words. For all that she had been a beast to him and made a fool of herself, Lieutenant Callaghan was there to dry her tears and give her comfort.

Shoving aside the pillows, Charity rolled onto her back, her eyes tracing the faint lines of the canopy as she considered the puzzle that was Lieutenant Callaghan. All those smiles and jests, yet he'd spoken of loneliness with the tone and feeling of one who knew the sentiment intimately. Yet time after time, he avoided the shadows of life. Feigning frivolity.

Curse Mama for interrupting. Every time Charity spoke with Lieutenant Callaghan, it felt as though she chipped away at those walls around his heart, bringing her closer to the whole of him. Then Mama had blundered in and swept her away.

A door slammed, reverberating through the house. Charity bolted upright, a hand to her chest, and she hurried to her bedchamber door. Wincing against the light, she searched the hall outside, but there was no sign of trouble. Then raised voices drew her to Papa's study door.

"Impossible! Do you wish us to be the laughingstock of the neighborhood?" cried Mama, her shrill voice piercing Charity's temple like an ice pick.

"That is precisely why we must leave! No one will be the wiser about our circumstances in a new town!"

Charity sighed. Why did her parents believe that a little bit of wood kept anyone from overhearing? Especially when they were bellowing like fishmongers. In truth, it was a miracle that news of Papa's failed investments hadn't made its way onto the gossipers' lips. Or perhaps they were too afraid to pass on the hearsay until Mama's downfall was certain; though many had no compunction in spreading half-truths or blatant falsehoods, no one would risk earning the dragon's wrath if it were merely wounded and not vanquished.

Retrench or retreat. Either option was bound to cause them heartache, but neither Mama nor Papa cared one jot for her opinion on the matter, so there was no reason to hover at the door. Having heard variations of it for months, Charity knew every thrust and parry of that battle.

Turning on her heels, she moved back to her darkened bedchamber when the sound of her name had her halting, her ears trained towards the door to hear Mama say, "It is the only match she will ever make—"

"But Honeyfield? The man is a letch!" said Papa.

"Yes, but he is very interested in her. We've found decent matches for the rest of our girls, but we cannot expect better for Charity when she refuses to repair her standing among society."

Papa huffed. "What about that navy chap—?"

"Why do you insist on speaking if you are going to only spout nonsense?" said Mama with a scoff. "He is in the Kingsleys' camp. I do not know what game he is playing, but he is only toying with her. Mr. Honeyfield is ready to make her an offer, and that will free up the funds we spend on her—"

"That is hardly going to make a difference! *You* are bleeding us dry, not our daughter!"

Eyes fixed on the door, Charity inched away, her throat tightening as she pressed a hand to her roiling stomach. Standing in the hall, she ignored the raised voices debating her worth as a wife and daughter, and for all that her head throbbed, it faded from her attention in favor of the aching pressure in her chest. Though her bedchamber called to her with promises of solitude and quiet, Charity couldn't bear the thought of being alone with these thoughts.

And there was only one person in the world who wished to be her friend.

...

Shifting the basket in her hands, Charity stared at the

ground just a few feet before her as she marched along the country lane, reciting again her speech.

"I thought I should bring you a gift..." she began and shook her head. Then attempting a more lighthearted tone, she said to the passing countryside, "You deserve a reward after listening to me whine and moan..."

The sun shone above her, unaware of her inner turmoil as it cast the world in brilliant, golden light. Her breath puffed out great clouds as she trudged along, her boots crunching against the frost-covered road. Catching the sound of an approaching carriage, Charity drifted to the farthest side, though there was little space for her; it was so much easier in the summer when one could traverse the fields and cut a more direct route, but the snow was just deep enough that she had to follow a clear path. The driver slowed and tipped his hat as they passed, but Charity hardly noticed as she mulled over what she might say to Lieutenant Callaghan. For all that he said he wished to be friends, she didn't know how to strike up a conversation.

Shifting the basket once more, she wished she hadn't been so zealous in packing it. Surely, a slice of spiced cake or a few biscuits would've sufficed as an excuse, and now, she was forced to heft the thing about.

"I thought I should apologize if I made you uncomfortable the other night," she said, holding up the basket, as though he were standing there before her. Shaking her head, Charity frowned. Was there any way she could speak to the fellow without looking like the lonely fool she was?

"Despite having known you for less than a fortnight, I was hoping to discuss a personal issue with you," she said with all the derision such a statement warranted. "Please, sir, I do not have any friends."

Sucking in a deep, chilly breath, Charity held her head high. She was not going to retreat now. Especially when Gladwell House loomed before her. With her luck, they'd seen her already; as much as her pride shuddered at the thought of knocking on the door, it blanched at the thought of them watching as she turned tail and ran away.

Charity gave the door a strong rap of her knuckles and straightened, holding her head high—and tried not to panic. Though she was quickly ushered into the parlor, matters weren't helped when she found not only the Ashbrooks but also the Kingsleys seated beside Lieutenant Callaghan. Two little boys sat at their feet, their blocks and toys scattered around them, but their parents all sat with stiff spines, their eyes watching her closely as she entered the room.

Only the lieutenant smiled when they all rose to their feet. Glancing back at the doorway, Charity tried to speak, but her mouth felt as though she'd drunk sand.

Lieutenant Callaghan stepped forward to greet her, and she shoved the basket at him, though he did not take it from her. Charity tried to swallow, but it was no use. Her gaze darted around at all the eyes staring at her.

"It's a token of gratitude," she finally managed.

"You didn't need to do that—" he began, but Charity plopped the basket in his hands and turned around, hurrying back the way she came.

"Miss Baxter," he called, his footsteps following after her, and she moved quicker, but when she paused to open the front door, Lieutenant Callaghan caught her and stepped in the way, so she could not leave. "Do not leave so soon."

Charity's eyes looked back down the hall to where the parlor door stood not five feet from here.

Lowering her voice, she whispered. "I only wanted to bring you a gift to thank you for your kindness at the Drakes' party. I am certain you didn't expect to spend your New Year's comforting a blubbering lady. And I wanted to apologize for Mama's behavior."

"Neither is necessary," he whispered back. "Are you feeling better?"

Unable to meet his gaze, Charity waved a dismissive hand. "I am well, of course—"

But she stopped, catching herself in that little white lie;

Lieutenant Callaghan avoided unpleasant realities enough, and if she wished for him to be honest with her, she needed to do so with him.

"In truth, I've had a rough go of it," she said with a pained smile. "I was hoping..." The words caught in her throat, and Charity shifted in place, eying the front door. "I wished to speak..."

Lieutenant Callaghan's lips pulled into a lazy grin, putting his dimples on full display. Irritating man that he was. "You came here, hoping to chat with me."

Charity huffed. "Yes, if you must know. You offered to be my friend, and I fear you are the only one wishing for the position at present."

"I am honored you came."

They stood thusly for several heartbeats, and Charity searched his expression for any hint of sarcasm, but Lieutenant Callaghan stood there, his hands tucked behind him, looking as pleased as he claimed to be.

Nodding towards the parlor, he whispered, "Would you please stay?"

But Charity's feet remained rooted in place. "That would be unpleasant for all involved."

"Not for me," he replied with a cheeky grin.

Charity wanted to grumble at that, but it was proving more and more difficult to hold on to her curmudgeon ways when faced with such sunniness.

"That may be the case, sir, but with our history, I cannot imagine spending even a quarter of an hour in that parlor."

Lieutenant Callaghan nodded, though he seemed entirely unmoved by her plight. "True, but the Kingsleys are good people, and I think you would feel better if you could heal the breach. Surely, it wouldn't hurt to try. Please."

And though all his arguments held quite a bit of weight to them, it was his simple but earnest plea at the end that had Charity agreeing. The man looked so determined to convince her that she couldn't deny him.

Turning back to the parlor, she struggled to put one foot in front of the other. Why had she agreed to this? Her pulse raced, and she forced herself to breathe as they moved towards the doorway. Surely, she could still flee, but she kept walking forward. Why had she allowed him to convince her to try?

Then his hand brushed at the small of her back, guiding her forward, and Charity sucked in a sharp breath.

Good heavens. She cared for him.

Chapter 11

That realization shot through Charity, skittering up and down her spine even as her skin warmed from his brief touch. She had feelings for Lieutenant Callaghan. Of course, that had been clear enough from their interactions, but those feelings had been irritation, anger, or even disgust. Charity had been willing to accept friendship, but when had it shifted to something pleasant? She hardly knew the man.

Thankfully, that realization held enough weight that Charity was too occupied with it to think about the Kingsleys. Lieutenant Callaghan divested her of their things and guided her to the sofa, and the group all took their seats (though the boys on the floor didn't notice any of it).

Only Mrs. Kingsley and Lieutenant Callaghan looked at her with anything nearing friendliness, though the former was far more forced than the latter. Mr. Kingsley held his daughter in his arms, rocking her with gentle movements while his eyes narrowed on Charity. The babe was snuggled in her papa's embrace, unaware of anything but the sweet dreams in her head. The Ashbrooks sat on the edge of their seats like warriors, awaiting the forthcoming battle.

Shifting in her seat, Mrs. Kingsley leaned forward and finally broke the silence. "From Lieutenant Callaghan's description, it sounds as though the Drakes' party was magnificent. How did you enjoy it?"

Charity stiffened, watching the lady. While there were pleasant moments, many had been quite the opposite. Had Mrs. Kingsley heard about the games? Charity doubted Lieutenant Callaghan would say anything, but there were plenty of others who were likely spreading the tale of how Miss Ingalls had embarrassed her. And then Mr. Honeyfield. Surely, people noticed his marked attentions.

Matters were not helped by all the glares boring into her, as though daring her to put one toe out of line.

"It was enjoyable," said Charity.

Then silence.

The boys continued to play, the elder building up towers of blocks while the younger swung his arms and sent them scattering. The quiet stretched on, only broken by the children's giggles as the toys skittered across the floor. Charity's face heated, and she longed for a fan to help cool her flushed skin.

Glancing at Lieutenant Callaghan, she wondered why the fellow was suddenly reticent, but he merely urged her one with a raise of his brows and a subtle nod towards the others.

With a quick look at the babe, Charity asked, "And who is this little miss?"

"Lily," said her papa as he watched Charity with narrowed eyes, as though expecting her to gobble the child up. She stiffened, fighting against the scowl that threatened to show itself.

Did he think her a monster?

How dare he sit there, full of righteous anger, when it was he who had hurt her! Mrs. Kingsley may have done nothing to earn the Baxters' scorn, but Mr. Kingsley was another matter altogether. True, Charity's behavior in the past was not what it ought to have been, but for the fellow to sit there, scowling at her like she was some ravening beast was ridiculous. It was not she who raised his expectations and then dashed them. It was not she who destroyed the other's reputation (however unintentionally). Charity's attempts to ruin his may have been purposeful—something she regretted dearly—but she hadn't succeeded. Yet, he clutched his child as though to shield her from Charity's taint

Mrs. Kingsley reached over and squeezed her husband's arm, though it did little to soften his expression.

Forcing herself to relax, Charity turned her attention to the lady. "I had heard you were blessed with a daughter. How old is she?"

Mrs. Kingsley smiled. "She is a year and a half old. And Oliver, there, is three. They are growing so quickly."

And more silence.

Charity glanced at Lieutenant Callaghan, barely containing her glower. He had insisted on this interlude, and it was clear they needed his vivacity if they were ever to get a conversation going, yet he sat there, mute and watching. With an encouraging smile, he nodded at her to continue. But what in the world could she say to the Kingsleys?

"And how are your parents?" asked Mrs. Kingsley.

Charity stiffened, her gaze shifting between the others while the lady's brows drew together. Surely, they hadn't heard anything. Plenty of townsfolk would pounce on any nugget that might taint the Baxter name, but she hadn't thought Mrs. Kingsley was one of them. Charity scoured the lady's words, searching for any sign of glee or smugness, but they seemed genuine enough.

And then Charity met Mr. Kingsley's eyes, which bore into her, hardening the longer the silence stretched. The Ashbrooks' expressions matched his, leaving Lieutenant Callaghan as the only one remotely pleased that she was there.

What was she doing here?

Charity jumped to her feet, and words tumbled from her mouth in a rush. "Pardon, but I fear I have stayed too long."

Turning away before the gentlemen had the chance to rise, Charity hurried out of the parlor, snatching her things from the peg beside the front door. Not pausing, she drew her cloak around her, fastening her bonnet on her head as Lieutenant Callaghan called after her. Charity didn't stop. Nor did she slow when his hand brushed her arm.

"What is the matter, Miss Baxter? Please do not leave so soon."

Charity shook her head, her feet continuing to march down the lane. "I am not going to sit there while the Ashbrooks and Kingsleys stare daggers at me. I am not the villain!"

Frowning, she let out a hard huff, the vapor swirling through the air. "It was not me who raised the other's expectations and then abandoned him to the vultures!"

Feet stomping against the ground, Charity laid out all his many sins, but it was not Mr. Kingsley who kept creeping into her thoughts. Again and again, Mrs. Kingsley came to mind. Her sitting so happily amongst her family. The defensiveness the others displayed on her behalf. Her beautiful son and daughter. The looks of adoration her husband sent her when he thought no one noticed.

A grand estate so prosperous that even a few poor seasons hardly depleted their coffers.

Stability. That word had seemed tedious and uninteresting in Charity's younger years. But then, her world had been full of it, with plenty to spare. Now, the only continuity in her life was knowing it was headed in a downward progression. Stability indeed.

Charity halted, her gaze staring off at the road ahead; Lieutenant Callaghan said something, but she didn't hear him as comprehension snapped into place with absolute clarity.

She was jealous of Mrs. Kingsley. That lady had everything—respect, love, and stability. Three things Charity had hunted for yet never attained, and with spinsterhood looming and her family's finances crumbling to ruin, it was clear she never would.

...

Miss Charity Baxter was as temperamental as an English summer. With rain one moment and sunshine the next, one needed to be prepared for any possibility. Though one might see a fine stretch for a while, only a fool thought it meant the sunshine would remain. And Thomas stood there, watching as Miss Baxter's clear skies filled with gusting winds and sheets of rain, washing away the firey lady and replacing her with that hollow creature he'd met at the Drakes' party.

Shrouded in the night as they had been, Thomas had only seen a faint shadow of it. Now, standing in the clear light of day, he watched the life drain from her gaze. Sorrow personified.

It resonated through him, drawing with it memories he'd thought were long forgotten. Yet despite his best efforts, they had been merely hidden away, ready to resurface at the slightest provocation. His heart ached as his pains flared anew, and he longed to do or say anything that might restore her spark. Fury or laughter, it didn't matter.

"It is a good thing you came for a visit," he said.

Miss Baxter's listless gaze turned to him, her brows rising in question.

"You see, I am in desperate need of a walk," he said. "I've been locked inside all day, and I need to stretch my legs. As much as I adore Scott, I can only read him so long."

"Sir Walter Scott?" she said.

"Is there any other?"

But Miss Baxter stood there, silent and blinking.

"You needn't be so surprised that I am literate," he said with a cheeky grin and a prayer that his jest would land properly this time.

Straightening, she frowned. "I am sorry. I did not mean to imply—"

"I am teasing, Miss Baxter."

"Perhaps if you warned me when you are going to be ridiculous, I might better appreciate the jest."

Thomas laughed, and a spark flashed in her eyes (which he

hoped was of the good variety). "If you always assume I am being ridiculous, you shall be right nine times out of ten."

"So says the man who spends his time reading the grand and sweeping works of Sir Walter Scott," she replied with a faint smile curling the edge of her lips. Thomas felt like preening.

Leaning closer, he lowered his voice to a conspiratorial whisper. "Do not tell a soul, but I am an avid reader."

"And you wish to keep your scholarly pursuits secret?" she asked, and Thomas motioned her along, leading them down the road.

"Of course. Otherwise, they may think me a sensible creature."

Miss Baxter's smile grew. "You may rest assured that even if you read heavy treatises all day long, I would think you the most foolish man I've ever met. But which of Scott's works do you enjoy the most?"

Thomas drew in a deep breath, tucking his hands behind him.

"The western waves of ebbing day
Rolled o'er the glen their level way;
Each purple peak, each flinty spire,
Was bathed in floods of living fire."

"*The Lady of the Lake*," she murmured.

Brows raised, he said, "You recognize the lines?"

"'...floods of living fire.' It's such a provoking description that it is hard to forget," said Miss Baxter. "Though it is far more impressive that you can recite it by memory. I have a gift for remembering in the short term, but the words fail me if I do not recite them daily. What is it about his poetry that you love so?"

Thomas studied the passing scenery. The world was awash in the same glowing light Scott had described as "floods of living fire." His thoughts sifted through his answer as he marveled at the beauty of the world around him.

"It is the way he takes mundane things, like a country view, and with a few scant words, he captures the inherent beauty, enhancing it into something truly extraordinary. He describes each detail with such passion, as though laying bare his very soul."

Miss Baxter smiled. "I wouldn't have taken you for a romantic, Lieutenant Callaghan."

Clearing his throat, Thomas shrugged. "A love of poetry does not make one a romantic. And I adore his novels equally. I am absolutely enamored with *Ivanhoe*. I've already read it four or five times, though that is also due to the lack of literature aboard the ship. I am forced to read the same novels and poetry again and again until we hit a port with a proper bookshop where I can replenish my stores."

"I've longed to read it," said Miss Baxter. "But I fear my allowance does not afford such luxuries, and I haven't a subscription to the lending library. What is it about?"

The pair wandered down the lane, and Thomas began to tell her the story of Wilfred and Rowena, and as much as he knew he ought not to give away the twists and turns of the tale, Miss Baxter kept prodding him along, and soon Thomas was lost in the telling of that epic story.

Their path meandered along, as did their conversation, and Thomas found himself smiling more and more. For all that they'd been thrown together several times over the past sennight and a half, little of their conversation had been of a serious bent. Yet now, they discussed books and poetry, which lead to tales of his time at sea, and Miss Baxter shared the little nothings of country life, which she clearly believed were inferior to his experiences, though Thomas loved each one.

But it wasn't merely the exchanging of ideas. Something in Miss Baxter relaxed him. That seemed a strange contradiction as the lady at his side was rarely calm. Thomas couldn't explain it, simply that they fell into step figuratively speaking as easily as they did literally. Like skilled dancers who knew how to navigate a ballroom, the conversation flowed easily, moving from one to the other as though they had known each other for many months, rather than days.

For all that she was a self-proclaimed curmudgeon, Miss Baxter was quite lively, and Thomas's heart grew light at the sight of her at ease in his presence, enlivening his spirits as no amount of jesting or teasing could do. It was a different sort of joy that sank deep into his heart. The sort of pleasure he hadn't felt since—

Thomas's thoughts halted in place. There was no good to be had in reminiscing about Patience.

Yet he couldn't turn away from those thoughts. Not that Miss Baxter reminded him of that lady—the two couldn't be more different in temperament—but the easy conversation. And the kinship he felt with her. Despite their surface differences, Miss Baxter felt like an old friend.

"What is that expression?" asked Miss Baxter with a narrowed look at him.

Thomas relaxed his features. "What expression?"

"It keeps cropping up as we wander along. I would call it pensive, but there is something more to it."

Tugging at the lapels of his greatcoat, Thomas shifted it on his shoulders and pulled the scarf tighter around his throat. "I was merely thinking about how much I am enjoying this conversation."

"Do you not find a vast array of scintillating discussions aboard a ship?"

"Oh, yes. We sit about discussing Scott at length, and once a row broke out over whether *Marmion* or *The Lady of the Lake* was his most compelling work. I am sorry to say that it resorted to fisticuffs and the captain banned all literary debates. My men were quite disheartened."

The corner of Miss Baxter's lips turned upward. "Ah, and here I thought you might pass a quarter of an hour without spouting inanities."

"I do not rely solely on inanities," replied Thomas with a mock scowl, modeled after Miss Baxter's. But the words struck him. Though it was a little thing, it brought to mind the many discussions he'd had of late that were as empty as Miss Baxter claimed.

"True," she replied. "You mix in a healthy dose of ridiculousness as well."

Thomas stepped in front of her and studied the lady with a solemn gaze. "Dear Miss Baxter, are you teasing me?"

The young lady arched a single brow and looked down her nose at him. "My dear Lieutenant Callaghan, I may not be as humorous as yourself, but that does not mean I am devoid of all levity. I have been known to say as many as three ridiculous things in a fortnight."

Smothering a laugh, Thomas met that with a look that was equally serious as he reached toward the stone wall edging the road. "Ah, yes. You are a model of frivolity."

Thomas took a handful of snow, packing it together with slow, purposeful movements while watching her intently. Miss Baxter glanced at the snowball, and her feigned indignity slipped, her eyes widening.

"You wouldn't dare."

But he gave her a broad grin in return. "One, two, three, four..."

Miss Baxter's eyes twitched between his gaze, the snowball, and the open lane.

"...five, six, seven..."

Before he reached eight, Miss Baxter took hold of her skirts and ran like a fox before the hounds. Speeding through the last numbers, Thomas launched the snowball on "ten!" and it flew through the air, smashing into her back.

Chapter 12

Scooping up a handful of snow, Miss Baxter pressed it quickly into a ball and launched it back at him, though it flew wide of its target. Darting down a crossroad, she ducked behind a wall; Thomas armed himself again and followed after, not bothering to hide his approach. She popped up and threw a great fistful at him, knocking his hat clean off, and before he knew what he was about, another hit him full in the face, the clumps of snow slithering down his cheeks.

Thomas wiped at his eyes to find Miss Baxter fleeing once more, her laughter ringing out in the winter's air. Slipping around a gate, she snuck into a nearby field, and he followed after, forcing himself not to run as her progress was difficult across the slippery surface. He allowed her to get ahead while preparing his ammunition.

"Oh, ho, are we going to play hide and seek?" he called as she disappeared into a copse of trees.

"A warrior knows when to go to ground."

In summertime, the spot would be quite hidden and secluded, indeed, but with the branches bare of leaves, Thomas saw well enough through the thickets. A flash of bonnet, and he sent a snowball flying, but she ducked, and it splattered against a trunk. Thomas hopped over a snow-covered rock and gave chase, following her further into the wilds.

Miss Baxter leapt from behind a tree as he passed, hitting him in the back of the head from a mere two feet away. Thomas whipped around to see her hurrying back the way she'd come; he chucked his snowball at her, and caught her in the shoulder, though it did nothing to slow her down as she disappeared once more.

Her cloak was a deep blue, which did not blend perfectly with her surroundings, but neither did it stand out enough to make a clear target—unlike his bicorn hat, which stood up like a flag, begging to be seen. In all honesty, it was a ridiculous bit of fashion in wartime, though infinitely better than the army's bright red, which served as a perfect target in a field filled with smoke and chaos.

A flash of blue, and Thomas darted to the right, fighting through the snow and thickets to find Miss Baxter in a clearing. The moment he came into view, she threw her weapons at him, but he dodged them easily.

"I see you are unarmed," he said with a smug smile, holding up his snowball for her to see.

Miss Baxter stiffened and looked around, though there was no way to arm herself before he got her. Stepping back, she put a large tree between them.

"That won't protect you," he said in a sing-song.

"You are forgetting something very important," she said, peeking out from behind it as he drew closer.

Thomas stopped within touching distance of the tree, so close that he couldn't miss. "And what is that?"

Miss Baxter gave him a wicked grin. "I hate to lose."

With that, she yanked on the branch above him with all her might, making the tree shudder. Thomas stared at her as she leapt away from the trunk, springing clear of the canopy. His feet moved when he realized what was coming, but they tangled over themselves, and he fell backward as the limbs dumped all their snow atop him.

His hat lay on the ground beside him, his great coat and scarf splayed out around him, and Thomas reached up to wipe at his face as snow and slush gathered in his nostrils and ears. And then the copse rang with laughter—or more accurately, cackling. Unreserved and undignified, Miss Baxter's mirth rang through the air, and Thomas couldn't help but join in. Especially when the young lady appeared above him, her face alight with her triumph.

"I hate to lose," she echoed.

"So I see."

Brushing off his face and chest, Thomas rose to his feet, and Miss Baxter made no move to help him, occupied as she was with crowing over him.

"Truce?" he asked, bending down to pick up his bedraggled hat.

"Is it the navy's policy to accept a truce from a vanquished foe?" she asked with mock innocence.

As the cascade of snow now provided ample ammunition for him to retaliate, Thomas was sorely tempted to begin another assault, but he couldn't bring himself to steal away the joy of her triumph; Miss Baxter beamed with it, glowing as brightly as the sun above.

"I concede defeat," he said with a low bow. "Though I warn you I have little to my name, so there is hardly any bounty to be claimed with your victory."

"Oh, the memory of your startled expression is bounty enough, Lieutenant Callaghan." Miss Baxter gave him another haughty lift of her nose and sauntered away.

Thomas laughed. Not a little, light thing, but something deep and rich as he ran to catch her. Offering up his arm, he helped her over the uneven ground until they made their way back to the road, looking quite the worse for wear, but all the happier for their excursion.

"My toes are frozen through," she murmured. "I should've worn sturdier boots, but I hadn't anticipated a flight through the woods."

"If you had remained on the road where it was clear your feet would be fine," he replied.

"And make myself a better target for you?"

Thomas hid a grin. Miss Baxter was such a mix of contrasting elements. So serious and sad, yet more and more, she was meeting his jests with humor, softening the edges of her hard exterior. He couldn't help but wonder what sort of woman she'd be if she hadn't been raised in the Baxters' home, amongst the cutthroat machinations of the social elite.

"And what brought you to my doorstep this afternoon?" he asked. "I cannot imagine you wished to chat with the Ashbrooks and Kingsleys."

Miss Baxter stiffened at his side, and Thomas glanced at her from the corner of his eye, cursing his wayward tongue as her brightness vanished, replaced by the cold detachment of a society lady. He wanted to lighten her expression once more, but though he played the fool at times, Thomas had learned his lesson. Miss Baxter did not always welcome being teased out of her severity.

Brow furrowed, she seemed to consider his question as they walked along, arm-in-arm. And it was several long moments before she ventured to answer.

"I was hoping to speak to a friend."

"And instead of solace, you found an uncomfortable situation," said Thomas with a wince. "I am sorry for that."

Miss Baxter shook her head. "It was not your doing."

"As I am the one who insisted you join us in the parlor, I deserve some of the blame," he replied, before shifting the conversation away from that fretful subject. "But I am willing and ready to hear anything you have to say."

Pulling him to a stop, the lady met his gaze with that worried twist of her brow on display as she studied him. "Do you truly wish to hear my troubles?"

Thomas almost spouted out a flippant answer, for why would he have said it if he hadn't meant it? But he knew it would frustrate her, rather than inspire further confessions, and more than anything, he wanted her to talk to him. He couldn't explain why, but knowing Miss Baxter considered him a confidant and friend filled him with a burning sense of pride. He didn't think she gave her trust easily, and yet she stood there, handing it to him.

"I do," he replied, meaning it as seriously as anything he'd ever said.

Miss Baxter's gaze softened, holding his for the briefest of moments before she nodded and turned away, continuing on their path. "Mama wishes me to marry Mr. Honeyfield because she is desperate to get me out of their home."

Everything inside him clenched at that declaration.

"And I am beginning to think that I ought to do as they say—"

"No." The answer was sharp and immediate.

Miss Baxter glanced at him. "But I am a financial burden to them, and if an opportunity is presented, isn't it my duty to accept? A son is not allowed to choose whether or not he wants a profession or even which he will pursue—"

"No."

That sharp answer garnered him another look, and Thomas fought not to squirm beneath her regard.

"There is a world of difference between being forced into a profession one despises and marrying a filthy letch of a man," he explained. "The only blessing in the latter is that he is likely to pass away while you are still young, but what you'd endure in the meantime is unthinkable. And that is assuming he is honorable enough to provide for you in his will or that he won't lose his fortune in the meantime, neither of which is guaranteed. To say nothing of the fact that you are risking your very life allowing that diseased creature anywhere near your person."

Miss Baxter shuddered, and he doubted it was from the cold. Raising his free hand, Thomas laid atop the one she had threaded through his arm, hoping the touch might give her some comfort.

"Surely, your situation is not as dire as that," he added.

With a heavy sigh, Miss Baxter began to speak. Thomas struggled to keep his thoughts to himself as she laid bare all the troubles in her heart, but if she was looking for solace with him rather than some long-standing friend, then she must not have anyone else to hear her woes. That settled in his chest with a spark of warmth that seemed wholly inappropriate for the situation. Certainly, he wasn't pleased that she had no one else to turn to, and it was humbling to think she turned to him only because she had no one else—but perhaps Miss Baxter would've chosen him regardless.

How long had it been since anyone spoke to him in such a manner? Sharing their troubles and looking to him for comfort? Thomas scoured his memory, but his heart shuddered as it wandered too close to subjects best left alone.

A smile sprung to his lips. Thankfully, Miss Baxter did not see it before Thomas recalled the serious nature of this discussion and tempered it into a more encouraging expression, and he hoped a touch ponderous. Something more appropriate for the occasion.

Forcing his attention back to Miss Baxter, Thomas nodded and gave those little sounds that demonstrated a listening ear, though he had no idea what else to say or do. Her troubles were not easily resolved, and he knew so little about the players involved.

"Even if I were to be brave enough to forge my own path and subject myself to the role of governess or companion, I know too much of what happens to those poor ladies. Surely, being at the mercy of employers, who can turn you out without a character reference for the slightest provocation, is no better than marrying a man—no matter how revolting—who is obligated to provide for you."

Before Thomas could point out one especially wretched aspect of marrying a man like Mr. Honeyfield, Miss Baxter hurried to add, "Fending off the advances of one letch must be better than all the masters who consider a governess's responsibilities broader than advertised. At least being a wife would give me more respectability and income than a governess."

And with that, Miss Baxter fell silent. For a moment, Thomas thought she awaited a response—though he had no idea what to say to such a conundrum—but the quiet was filled with weighty thoughts as she lost herself in her head.

Then Miss Baxter pulled him to a stop and met his gaze. "Have you ever felt trapped and at the mercy of others' decisions, unable to forge your own path? Longing for something different, but the only other possibilities are equally dire?"

Thomas's mouth grew dry as those hazel eyes bore into his, filled with such desperation, as though his answer held utmost importance to her happiness and well-being. And his heart ached.

It had been some three and twenty years, and many of the memories had faded from his mind, but Thomas still felt that dark hole in his heart as he recalled his parents walking away from his ship, uncertain if he would ever see them again. Many thought nine was old for a boy's education to begin, but Thomas knew it was far too young to be torn away from his family and tossed aboard a ship. His parents had regaled him with tales of the sea and the adventures that would await him, and Thomas wasn't certain if they had been willfully ignorant or lied, for the navy was nothing like the swashbuckling tales they'd shared.

Thomas's brow furrowed, and he considered all that while Miss Baxter watched him with expectant eyes, pleading with him to validate her pain. Despite her frigid exterior, there was such an openness to her, and it called to him.

"Yes, but I've learned to look for the good in every situation," he said, forcing a smile. "It does no good to wallow in what cannot be changed."

Miss Baxter huffed, the edge of her lips twisting into a mirthless grin. "I suppose I could say that either option would take me far from here, allowing me to begin again. A fresh start is something of a blessing."

"Ah, there you go. Whenever you catch of whiff of Mr. Honeyfield's rancid breath, simply think to yourself, 'I could be stuck in a room with the harpies of Bristow society,'" he replied with a teasing tone.

The jest was not his best, but Charity smiled, nonetheless. Lieutenant Callaghan was keen to hide solemn truths behind silly expressions, so why couldn't she? But her eyes searched his for cracks in that façade. The barrier was strong between them, keeping her out as thoroughly as the stone walls on the side of the lane, but Charity swore the mortar was crumbling.

But Lieutenant Callaghan offered his arm again, and they continued on their way, his conversation as substantive as the puffy clouds above. He filled the air with larks, retreating behind his usual nonsense. Gone was the man who discussed poetry with the fire and passion of a true romantic, who reveled in the grand tales of love and loss that were rife in Scott's work. A man could not adore such sentimental tales and feel nothing. Charity sensed it lurking beneath the laughter, and she longed to find some way to reach into his heart. To see the whole man.

Her home came into view, and she was no closer to understanding what he was hiding or why; she had bared her troubles to him, but Lieutenant Callaghan gave her nothing in return. Charity's steps dragged as they drew closer to Juniper Court, but there was no point in remaining with him if he was only going to retreat behind his jester persona.

"I thank you for a grand afternoon out," said Lieutenant Callaghan, sweeping into another low bow after he deposited her on her doorstep. "You are a worthy adversary, and I hope to test my skill against yours once more in the field of battle."

But Charity didn't smile. His own stiffened, and he straightened, popping his hat back on his head. Then with a few mumbled words, Lieutenant Callaghan turned tail and scurried away, and she watched him as he disappeared down the lane. Though there was so much evidence to the contrary, her heart could not ignore the glimpses of the serious man inside the fool. Heaven help her, she was determined to discover him.

Chapter 13

It seemed strange that the final day of the Christmas season was the grandest. The past twelve days had been filled with endless parties and gatherings, ensuring that every member of the gentry was well and truly exhausted for the largest and most elaborate of the nights. Granted, if it were reversed, beginning with the most lavish parties would only make the other pale in comparison. Charity supposed it was merely proved the Twelve Days of Christmas ought not to be crushed full of gatherings.

The Nelsons had spared no expense with the decorations, ensuring their Twelfth Night festivities would be talked of for months after. With so much of their home gilded and covered in frescoes, the rooms required little ornamentation, but their hosts had draped every corner of the drawing room with white flowers and greenery. The walls and ceilings were busy things, and the addition of the decorations was a tad too much for Charity's tastes, even if it was impressive.

She glanced around the room, but there was no sign of a clock. Surely, she was not the only one who was ready for a long rest. Thankfully, the evening would not drag onto the wee hours of the morning.

Goodness, their hosts had even dragged away the majority of the chairs, leaving the space mostly empty except for an elaborate set of armchairs, which were draped in velvet like makeshift thrones. Candles burned in every inch of the room, bathing them in light and opulence, ensuring that every guest knew just how much expense the Nelsons had incurred for the evening.

But it was lost on Charity, for her attention was entirely fixed on the naval uniform striding into the gathering. She couldn't help but smile, though she managed to keep it to something more polite than eager, despite her feet wanting to hurry to Lieutenant Callaghan's side.

"My friends decided to forgo tonight's party, but I couldn't bring myself to stay at home when I suspected you might be here," he said, coming up beside her.

"Thank goodness, for I am in desperate need of cheering," replied Charity.

"Surely, you are not unhappy on Twelfth Night," he said with mock shock. "It is against the rules for anyone to be morose at such a time."

"Then they ought to guarantee that everyone has at least one designated companion. Without you, I am cursed to stand by myself the entire time."

"Ah, so I am required to remain by your side and keep you entertained?"

But any response Charity might've given (and it was unlikely to have been as witty as she would've liked) was interrupted when Mr. Nelson raised his voice to the group, welcoming them to the celebrations. Soon, he and Mrs. Nelson were walking about the group with outstretched bowls for the ladies and gentlemen. Each guest picked a slip of paper from their respective bowls, reading out the parts assigned to them for the party, and Charity watched Mrs. Nelson drawing ever closer to her.

"Do you dislike Twelfth Night games?" whispered Lieutenant Callaghan.

"Pardon?"

"You look like you're facing the gallows."

"I am no good at being silly," she replied. "I always feel out of sorts when asked to do so."

Lieutenant Callaghan leaned closer and winked. "Ah, but you have a designated companion tonight, and I assure you I am talented enough for the both of us."

Charity sucked in a deep breath, relaxing her expression, and nodded as Mrs. Nelson stepped forward, shaking the ladies' bowl at her. Reaching in, Charity swirled the folds of paper. She didn't know if the Almighty cared about such frivolous things, but she sent a silent petition nonetheless that she might be granted a good role to play for the evening.

Plucking the paper free, she unfolded it and read,

"Miss Frumpish doesn't like in merry parties to mix;
Because she's as cross as two old sticks."

Charity stumbled over the last few words, stiffening as the others in the gathering snickered, sending her sly looks while tittering one betwixt the other. Where the rest were granted roles contrary to their personality, Miss Charity Baxter had been assigned the perfect one. If she were to ascribe to Lieutenant Callaghan's philosophy, she would call it a blessing as it required little playacting. But it was difficult to hold onto that good humor when the laughter lingered too long.

Lieutenant Callaghan nudged her as Mrs. Nelson moved along, and Charity forced herself to meet his gaze. "They are not laughing at you."

"Yes, they are."

Considering that, he shrugged. "And what of it? Embrace the role you've been given. A little dose of ridiculousness never hurt anyone."

But Mr. Nelson appeared before him, offering up the gentlemen's bowl, and Lieutenant Callaghan snatched up the first paper he touched. With a quick perusal, he flashed Charity a dimpled smile before reading aloud,

"I am Sir Harry Hard-to-Please, and never in my life
Have I beheld a woman good enough for my wife."

That earned another burst of raucous laughter, which Lieutenant Callaghan spurred on by puffing out his chest and strutting about, giving every lady in the room a gimlet eye. Turning back to Charity, he met her furrowed look with an expectant one, his eyes sparking with mirth and begging her to join in.

"Miss Frumpish, would you care to take a turn about the room with me?" he asked in a tone dripping with haughty disdain.

Charity glanced at the others as each adopted their part, many of which were jesters, windbags, or flirts. Biting her lips, she tried to think of something to say, her thoughts struggling for anything. When she looked at Lieutenant Callaghan, he merely stood there, awaiting her with his arm outstretched, his gaze begging her to join in.

Taking in a deep breath, Charity straightened, raising her nose high in the air, and batted away his arm. "How dare you, sirrah! Taking a turn with a gentleman is too like dancing, and I cannot bear to take part in such vulgarity, Sir Hard-to-Please."

Lieutenant Callaghan hid a laugh behind a cough, and replied, "Too true, Miss Frumpish. Too true. The ballrooms are full of ladies who think themselves so light on their feet, but they stagger about like drunken elephants. Disgraceful!"

A chuckle eked out, and Charity forced it back, matching her partner's sneer as she shuddered. "Positively dreadful!"

"I think it best if we notify Our Majesties of this travesty!" he said, nodding towards the thrones where the Twelfth Night King and Queen held court.

"Of course, you are right, Sir Hard-to-Please," said Charity, though he had to drag her towards the makeshift dais. With paper crowns atop their heads, Mrs. Thackeray and Mr. Bright sat in their thrones, greeting each of the guests who deigned to petition them for their royal favor.

Lieutenant Callaghan swept forward in a deep bow. "Miss Frumpish and I have been discussing matters and have urgent business that must be seen to, Your Majesties."

Mr. Bright rose an imperious brow. "And what is that Sir Hard-to-Please?"

The fellow glanced over his shoulder at Charity, and she felt rooted to the place, struggling to know what to do. So, she began with a curtsy that was too shallow to be counted as such.

"I..." Charity frowned and struggled through the mess her thoughts were making at the moment. "This party must end posthaste. It is entirely too raucous! And the hour. Do you know it is nearly eight o'clock? We must be abed!"

That pronouncement was met with a few laughs, though it was hardly encouraging, and Mrs. Thackeray straightened, breaking her regal character to stare at Charity, which did nothing for her equilibrium.

But Lieutenant Callaghan popped upright again and nodded vigorously, calling out with a booming voice. "This party is a disgrace. I would think the Nelsons would invite handsome women. The ladies here are all scarecrows. Gangly and awkward. And with a dreadful sense of fashion. Positively wretched!"

Glancing around the room, he studied each lady and gave a particularly lovely gown a frown, snatching his handkerchief from his pocket and holding it to his nose as though the sight of it was bound to make him faint.

"It offends the sensibilities something dreadful," he moaned, which earned him heartier laughs. "At the very least they ought to be sent home and smarten up a bit. They cannot expect to find husbands or please the ones they have if they go about in public looking like ragamuffins."

But the king blustered at that, pointing at the pair. "Such impertinence! Off with their heads!"

"Come, Miss Frumpish," said Lieutenant Callaghan with wide eyes. "We must flee!"

Charity couldn't help the laugh, especially when the rest of the room erupted with it as he snatched her by the arm and hurried her away from the throne.

The pair moved about the room, insulting everyone they came across, yet each of Lieutenant Callaghan's pronouncements was met with laughs as the other players answered back as their character ought. Charity tried to match her partner, but it was difficult to think of what to say when she was so occupied by him, his eyes alight with a laugh meant only for her. Taking his arm, she forced a grimace on her face and followed him about, reveling in each ridiculous moment.

Chapter 14

"Are you finished yet?" asked Thomas, employing Sir Hard-to-Please's snobbish inflection.

"You are a child," murmured Miss Baxter (though her tone was entirely her own). "It's been hardly a quarter of an hour."

"Surely not, I am certain it has been at least three times that long." Thomas shifted in his seat.

"Be still!" she hissed.

With his back straight against the chair, Thomas stared forward; the light from the candle at his left blocked out much of his view of that side of the room, and the screen behind which Miss Baxter sat was to his right, leaving the world ahead as his only distraction. Another pair were similarly situated not far from them, with the lady sitting for the gentleman as he sketched the shadow her profile cast across his screen.

This room was far quieter than the rest, with the occupants gathered in quiet conversations or more sedate games, and Thomas's gaze kept drifting toward Miss Baxter. He could not see her behind the screen, but there was no mistaking the occasional smothered laugh as she set about sketching his profile.

His heart lightened at the thought of her smile. Making others merry was easy enough and hardly worth noting—he swanned, eliciting laughter wherever he went—but Miss Baxter was far more discerning in her joy, giving it only when he'd truly proven his mettle.

"Do you wish to see my work?" she asked, so Thomas stood and came around to her side of the screen to find the most hideous profile ever drawn. A big forehead sloped down into a nose, which looked more porcine than human. Thick lips that were puckered into a sneer, but worst of all was the bald sweep of his head that showed only a few scraggly bits of hair combed over the naked top.

"It is an exact likeness, don't you think?" she said, gazing at him with feigned innocence. Then turning to a passing gentleman, she added, "What say you, Sir Harry Hoax?"

Mr. Talbot stopped and glanced at the page, his brows rising.

"Do you not think it is a fine likeness of Sir Hard-to-Please?" she prodded.

The gentleman hesitated a moment too long, and Miss Baxter's smile slackened, but before Thomas could leap in to aid her, Mr. Talbot nodded.

"Oh, certainly, Miss Frumpish. I've never seen a more accurate profile drawn. You are immensely talented."

That she was, for though it bore no resemblance to reality, the surety of her lines and the way she'd distorted his features showed genuine skill. Thomas almost wanted to sit for another and see what she could do in earnest.

"Miss Lydia Lollipop," called Mr. Talbot, stopping another young lady. "Stop a moment and marvel at this bit of perfection."

Mr. Talbot held up Miss Baxter's drawing, and Miss Lollipop (Thomas could not recall what her true name was) burst into giggles.

"Quite right, sir," she managed between bouts of laughter. "Especially the hair."

"Yes, well, it does help that the subject is such a handsome fellow," said Thomas, puffing out his chest.

"True," said Mr. Talbot. "But that is what makes it all the more impressive. It is difficult to capture such perfection, yet Miss Frumpish has managed to do so."

But Miss Baxter did not join in their chuckles, and Thomas glanced over to find her staring at the parlor doorway, her cheeks paling. There stood Mrs. Baxter and Mr. Honeyfield as they searched the gathering. Without waiting to ask, Thomas grabbed Miss Baxter by the arm and yanked her behind Mr. Talbot.

"Stay there," hissed Thomas, when the chap tried to turn and see what had spurred him to action. Then Thomas nudged Miss Lollipop nearer until she formed a wall with Mr. Talbot.

"What is going on?" But Mr. Talbot had the good sense to keep his voice low.

"You are rescuing a damsel in distress," said Thomas, glancing around Mr. Talbot.

Miss Lollipop looked over her shoulder and blanched when she saw Mr. Honeyfield. "Whatever you require, sir."

"Follow behind us until we are safely out," he said, nodding towards the door opposite of them. Mr. Talbot frowned but followed Miss Lollipop's lead, and Thomas hurried Miss Baxter towards the exit, not stopping until they were safely in the hall.

"My thanks," called Thomas from over his shoulder as they abandoned the others and ducked into a nearby alcove.

"It will do no good," said Miss Baxter with a heavy sigh. "One way or another they will find us."

"One ought not to cry defeat before the battle has begun in earnest," said Thomas, peering out to see Mrs. Baxter and Mr. Honeyfield turning down the hall, away from this hiding place. Taking Miss Baxter by the hand, he hurried her along in the opposite direction, slipping into the first open room they came upon.

From a quick look, it seemed to be a sitting room of some sort, full of chairs and sofas that looked more decorative than inviting. This side of the room was empty, though card tables stood at the far end with ladies and gentlemen laying out their wagers and crowing over their victories. Wandering to the sofa, Miss Baxter sat down and faced the fireplace, staring into the crackling flames. Still clutching her drawing, her shoulders slumped, her eyes unfocusing as she watched the yellow and orange light dance across the last vestiges of the Nelsons' yule log.

Sitting beside her, Thomas took her drawing in hand and smiled at the image that perfectly captured the spirit of Sir Hard-to-Please.

"I do not know what to do about Mr. Honeyfield," she murmured. Then turning her gaze to him, she added, "But then, I do not know what to do about you, either."

Thomas's brows rose. "Must you do something about me?"

Miss Baxter's eyes looked far older than her years, weighed down by such cares, and Thomas longed to see them brighten once more.

"Tell me something true, Lieutenant Callaghan."

"The earth is a sphere that rotates around the sun, taking a full three hundred and sixty-three days to make the journey—"

Miss Baxter scoffed, that pert little sound bringing a smile to Thomas's lips, for though her eyes narrowed on him, they held at least a spark of something more than despair and resignation.

"Something specific to you," she said. "I have told you so much about myself, but I fear I know little about you."

Thomas's mouth opened, but nothing came out. Forcing his fingers to relax, he set the drawing to one side to keep it from crinkling any further.

"For example, where is your family from? You must have a mother and father, but do you have any siblings?" she prodded.

"As I've said before, I'm from the North—"

"Oh, yes. That paints a clear picture."

Thomas almost cracked a smile at her dry tone. "Northumberland. A little town of no consequence not far from the Scottish border."

But Miss Baxter merely waited with raised brows as though expecting more. Thomas shifted in his seat.

"Like all creatures, I have a mother and a father. And last I heard I have eight siblings." Thomas glanced at the doorway. "We'd better keep an eye on the hall. At some point, your mother is bound to come searching here."

"You've heard me speak at great length about so many personal subjects, yet am I to receive only the most basic of responses, Lieutenant Callaghan?"

Thomas shrugged. "There is little to say. I joined the navy when I was nine, so they are little more than strangers to me."

Miss Baxter tensed, her spine straightening. "Surely, you write to them. My siblings may be scattered to the winds, but—"

"My father never bothered to write, and my mother does so maybe twice a year. My siblings were far too young to do so when I left and haven't adopted the habit now that they're grown. As I haven't clapped eyes on them since I was a lad, there seems little point in striking up a conversation now."

Though the lady did not give any great gasp at that declaration, Thomas felt her shock as she stared at him.

"You haven't seen them since you were a lad?" she asked. "Did you never return home during your shore leave?"

Thomas sighed. There was little point in rolling about in the past like a pig in the mud, but he knew Miss Baxter well enough to recognize that stubborn set of her jaw. The lady would not leave it alone until he gave some explanation. So be it.

"My parents were romantics and thought all they needed was love to be happy. They married, despite their families' objections, and found themselves cut off and unable to navigate the world without their parents' aid. But they soldiered on and soon were saddled with a horde of children with no way to pay for them. So, they abandoned me to the navy and went on with their lives. They couldn't afford to send money for me to make the journey, and even if they had, I often didn't have time enough ashore to make the trip from Portsmouth or Liverpool—

"

"No."

Thomas's brows rose. "I know my own history, Miss Baxter, and I am speaking the truth."

"Why do insist on this charade?"

"Charade?"

Her eyes narrowed, and her brow furrowed, though her expression held not the usual bite of true displeasure. "You speak flippantly, but I do not believe it. I feel the truth lurking there beneath your feigned indifference, Lieutenant Callaghan. There is no harm in feeling betrayed or hurt or abandoned."

Miss Baxter's gaze held his in an implacable hold, refusing to allow him to look away, though Thomas longed to. It was a story he'd told a few times before, but usually, it was met with a nod and a polite change of topic—not a verbal assault.

"I am not the only man whose family tossed them into the navy. It's common enough for people to ship off their sons—"

"No," she repeated, emphasizing it with a shake of her head. "Tell me to mind my business or that you do not wish to speak of it, but do not pretend it is of no importance to you."

Thomas tried to look away, but he was trapped there in her hazel depths. The Miss Baxter he'd first met was not a sentimental or overly emotional person, but in that gaze, he saw the fire and passion burning in her heart. It rang with truth and determination, echoing her words, and sparking within his chest.

Only the touch of her hand wrenched him free of her gaze. Thomas hadn't realized his fingers had been tapping out a rapid beat against the floral upholstery until she forced them to still. Miss Baxter rested hers atop his, and though both their hands were encased in silk and linen, the heat of her skin seeped into his. Thomas stared at their joined hands.

"You are very kind, Miss Baxter, but I learned long ago that the world is a lonely place. You would do best to guard your heart against such sentimentality, or it will be broken again and again."

"Is that why you offered to be my friend, Lieutenant Callaghan? So I will learn to be an island unto myself?"

The sarcasm in her tone drew Thomas's gaze to hers, but that flash of humor faded as a tender smile played at the corner of her lips. And once more, he was captured by her gaze (though he was still keenly aware of the feel of her hand against his). Yes, the Miss Baxter he'd thought her to be was nothing like the creature seated beside him. Concern twisted her brows and her eyes shone with it, reaching deep into his soul and touching it as veritably as her hand touched his.

Others must have absconded with the candlesticks, for this portion of the room was dark except for the fireplace blazing before them. The light played off Miss Baxter's features, shifting and dancing as easily as this mercurial lady's moods. It caught the green in her eyes, reminding him of trees in springtime when the buds began to sprout, covering their brown branches in a haze of green and filling the forests with the promise of new life and new beginnings.

Thomas didn't know when he'd drawn so near to her, but it felt as though the space between them was still too vast, despite their faces being mere inches from each other. Like catching a glimpse of shore after weeks adrift at sea, Miss Baxter called to him, luring him closer with promises of home and comfort. Those eyes, which saw him so clearly, held his, and Thomas leaned closer, his lips brushing hers in a whisper of a touch.

Laughter from behind them snapped Thomas upright, jerking away as the card tables at the far end of the room erupted with jeers and cheers in equal measures. Everything inside him recoiled, his memory dredging forth all the many reasons why being so near a lady in any sense was a mistake of the highest order. Never again. Not ever.

Yanking free, Thomas leapt to his feet and crossed to the mantle.

Chapter 15

Muscles tightening, Charity blinked at the man who had so nearly kissed her. That had happened, hadn't it? Or had she imagined that flutter against her lips? Having never been touched in such a manner, she rather thought she hadn't dreamt it, for it felt as though every nerve in her body had sparked to life for the first time.

She pressed a hand to her mouth, though it couldn't capture the touch, faint though it had been. Charity knew she ought to feel some flush of shame or discomfort at the very least, for though the others in the room were more enamored with their entertainments than what she and Lieutenant Callaghan had almost done, they had an audience of sorts. This certainly wasn't the time or place for such a display.

But what did it mean? Her thoughts raced with the possibilities. Was this the beginning of something new? Charity stared at his back as the fellow stood at the mantle, his gaze fixed on the flames, and she willed him to say something. In an instant, her mind conjured a dozen different scenarios, branching out into a dozen different futures. There were troubles aplenty in each of them, for courting a navy man was fraught with logistical issues, but surely, they could find a solution. If—

Lieutenant Callaghan shook his head and laughed, and for once, it held no mirth in it. It was curt and bitter, slicing through Charity's romantic delirium like a machete.

"If you think I am to be your savior from Mr. Honeyfield, you are greatly mistaken, Miss Baxter."

Charity's brows rose, and she longed for him to turn and face her. "Pardon?"

Another scoff. "Do not try to catch me, for I shan't be snared."

"That was never my intention," she replied with a frown.

Lieutenant Callaghan pushed off the mantle and finally turned to meet her, his arms crossed and a brow raised in challenge. "It wasn't? If we were caught in a compromising situation, you would land yourself a husband, placing you well out of reach of Mr. Honeyfield."

Charity gaped, fire flashing in her heart as she began to speak. But a spark of something in his eye held her tongue. The fellow deigned to meet her straight on for only a heartbeat before he turned his gaze away, and the stiffness in his shoulders seemed all wrong for the haughty demeanor he was showing.

"What are you doing, Lieutenant Callaghan?"

He smirked, but there was a hollowness to it that had her gaze narrowing. "I am merely setting the record straight, Miss Baxter. I offered friendship—not marriage vows. Stop throwing yourself at me."

Sucking in a deep breath, Charity tried to calm the fire burning in her heart, forcing herself to hold fast to the instincts warning her that things were not as they seemed. She had no more than the barest flashes of insight to go on, but she trusted them far more than this haughty demeanor he affected. Lieutenant Callaghan was an excellent actor, but he was acting all the same.

"I do not understand what is happening, but do not think you can lay all the blame on me." Charity watched him closely, trying to piece together the strangeness of this moment with every stray look and movement.

The fellow scoffed again, and Charity wanted to stuff a stocking in his mouth to stop him from doing so in the future. Then his gaze narrowed on her, and she felt as tiny and insignificant as an insect beneath his boot.

"You would lecture me about not blaming others? That is a laugh. You've spent nearly a decade laying all your troubles on the Kingsleys' shoulders—"

"That is not true!" she said, rising to her feet. "I am well aware that my behavior has been despicable in the past—"

"And yet you cling to your anger. Perhaps you ought to spend more time putting your words into practice rather than lecturing me. Do not be a hypocrite, Miss Baxter."

Charity sucked in deep through her nostrils, glaring at him as she let it out. Only when she was certain she could speak without shouting did she answer that accusation.

"I am no hypocrite, but I am human, Lieutenant Callaghan. I may espouse beliefs without perfectly embodying them." The gentleman opened his mouth to respond, but Charity stepped closer and hurried on. "Stop avoiding the subject, and stop trying to distract me by picking an argument! Every time our conversation drifts anywhere near a tender subject, you avoid it like the plague. I do not know why you do so, but don't you dare pretend as though that almost kiss was solely my doing."

His eyes widened for a moment. It was as quick as a hummingbird's wing, but Charity saw it. A flash of something genuine— and steeped in fear. She didn't understand it, but she refused to question it, either.

"I do not understand what you are doing, and if you do not want me, that is your prerogative. But please stop lying and deflecting." Charity held his gaze, hoping he would feel the truth, though he refused to give honesty in return. Her chest tightened, but she forced herself to add in a whisper, "I feel something growing between us—"

"No."

Frost reached its icy fingers into her heart at his hard tone. Lieutenant Callaghan crossed his arms, stepping away from her as his head haughtily raised in a pose that looked far more at home on her than him.

"I am never going to marry, Miss Baxter, so get that firmly out of your head. If you've imagined anything more than friendship, that is your doing, not mine. I have no obligation to you or anyone, so do not think to force one upon me—"

"That is not what I am doing!"

Lieutenant Callaghan smirked. "Isn't it? I merely wish to enjoy my evening, and you are going on about love and romance and who knows what else."

Turning away, he moved to the door, and Charity stared after him, unable to comprehend how the world had gone so topsy-turvy. But still, that fear in his eyes called to her, whispering to her that there was more to this sudden shift than it seemed. Clinging to those instincts, she followed him into the hall.

"Why must you always run away whenever things get the slightest bit serious?" she said, halting him in his tracks. Lieutenant Callaghan turned to face her, his arms folded tight across his chest. Gathering her courage close, Charity straightened, meeting his hard gaze with her own. "Anytime we speak of anything tender or personal, you run away and hide behind a laugh or a jest. And now, you are literally fleeing. I do not understand!"

Lieutenant Callaghan huffed, his expression devoid of any feeling as he studied her with cold eyes. "Then let me make it clear to you, Miss Baxter. I have tried to be patient with you, but I have reached my limit. I am done being your friend. Go pester someone else."

Turning on his heel, he marched away, calling over his shoulder. "A word of advice, Miss Baxter. If you wish to make and keep companions, you'd best stop being so bothersome."

The words struck their intended target, slamming into her heart with such force that Charity couldn't breathe. Pressing a hand to her middle as though that might staunch the blood drawn, she stared after him as he strode away without looking back.

Again and again, that precious near kiss played through her mind, and she dissected those few seconds before Lieutenant Callaghan had leapt away like she was on fire. But no matter how many times she reviewed it, Charity couldn't attribute it to herself. She had been the one to hold his hand, true, but he had leaned closer. He had gazed at her with that look every young lady longed to see—all full of desire and longing.

Lieutenant Callaghan had wanted to kiss her. Charity would stake great piles of money on it. So, what had she done to chase him away?

Pain pulsed through her, and Charity curled inward, wrapping her arms around her middle. Tears gathered in her eyes, but she sucked in a deep breath and stepped back into a darkened alcove. But when she realized this was where they'd hidden just minutes ago, Charity jerked back out of the space. She cast her gaze right and left, but there was nowhere else to hide, and her tears flowed faster than she could wipe them away.

Pressing her hands to her mouth, she tried to calm her breath, but her lungs hitched. Shaking her head, Charity gathered the last of her reserve, pulling her self-control tight around her. It hid the tears, but it could do nothing to mend the fractures in her heart.

But with that moment of calm came clarity. Whatever he may say or do or however he might lash out, Charity knew the truth. His words had been about his shortcomings—not hers. That did little to ease the sting, but it helped her to regain her composure.

Lieutenant Callaghan was a coward.

Chapter 16

Standing atop the hill's crest, Charity stared out at the expanse of white stretching around her. The weather had warmed enough to melt away much of the snow, but a sudden chill the night before had brought with it a new dusting, blanketing the gray and brown in a pristine layer of white. Thick clouds above felt like a quilt, all comfortable and cozy despite the nip in the air that turned her nose a bright red.

Some part of her wished to remain in that exact place until the sun drifted low over the horizon, lighting the world in oranges, pinks, and purples. But that would only extend her torture.

A sennight was not such a long time. If one were to consider a life in its entirety, seven days was little more than a heartbeat, yet much could happen in that short period. Three weeks ago Lieutenant Callaghan had crashed into Charity's life, altering every aspect of it. And the sennight since their last meeting had brought with it clarity. Lieutenant Callaghan may be a wretch, a traitor, and a fool of the highest order, but he was correct in one thing. Once the initial shock of their argument had faded, Charity's thoughts kept returning to one indisputable fact.

Which is how she found herself standing on the road with

a basket of goodies in hand. If she kept using sweets to soften apologies, Charity ought to learn how to make cakes and baskets, for the Baxters' larder was running low on both.

Cold seeped into Charity's toes, and she forced herself to walk again, moving down the country lane as her mind replayed her speech. Not that it would do any good, for she was bound to babble like a Bedlamite once the moment presented itself, but it gave her something to think about—other than nerves or Lieutenant Callaghan.

Odious man.

Charity scowled at the road ahead and forced her thoughts to the subject at hand. Perhaps nerves were better than anger, for the latter would not help her cause. This needed to be done. It must. It had taken her seven days to gather her courage, and she wasn't going to retreat now. The drive came into view, and Charity followed it along, reciting her speech. Speak the words, hand over the basket, and leave. Simple.

Avebury Park was a proud Elizabethan building. Though some alterations had been made to the original façade, it retained much of its former glory. Mr. Kingsley's father and grandfather had eschewed the trends that had families pulling down perfectly lovely estates to build Grecian-inspired squares, which looked identical to all the other columned exteriors. Charity rather liked the building; though not as ornamented as some, all the chimneys and vertical bits on top drew the eye upward, making it look so much taller and grander than the squat Georgian houses.

Admiring the house was a pleasant enough distraction, but soon the bell was pulled, the door was answered, and the guest was ushered in. With the difficulties between their families, Charity never visited the Park, and it surprised her to find the interior far different than its exterior. Though the family hadn't bothered to rebuild the house in the new style, someone had gone to great lengths to redesign the interior to match the changing fashions, which had moved from dark woods to lighter colors.

The effect was quite lovely. Where the entry would've felt far more cramped before, it was light and open. And when the footman led her into the parlor, Charity was astonished to find that the room was as airy as the rest.

But then she spied its master and mistress standing at the far end of the room, watching her, and the air left her lungs. Mouth dry, Charity stepped forward and curtsied. But when she straightened again, she stood there, blinking at the pair. And they stared back. Mr. Kingsley watched her with narrowed eyes, so she ignored him and approached the more welcoming of the pair.

With the basket lifted before her, Charity handed it to Mrs. Kinglsey. "I came to bring you this."

Her husband's frown deepened, and Charity held back the scowl that threatened to emerge. Could he not even accept a gift without suspicion? But before her thoughts traveled too far down that bitter path, Charity reined them in and turned to the purpose of her visit.

"Would you like a seat?" asked Mrs. Kingsley, but Charity shook her head.

"I only came to offer an apology," she tried to swallow, but her throat was so wretchedly dry! Forcing air into her lungs, Charity quickly added in one long breath, "I am sorry for how I have behaved to both of you, and though I hope you will accept my humblest apology, I do not expect or require it. I simply needed you to know I regret what has transpired between us."

Mr. Kingsley openly gaped, and Mrs. Kingsley's brows rose, the pair staring at Charity as though she were the featured attraction in a menagerie.

"That is all," she said with a quick bob before turning on her heel. Eyes fixed on the exit, Charity hurried away, only pausing once Mrs. Kingsley called after her. Turning around to face the lady, Charity found the pair striding toward her.

"Do forgive me, Miss Baxter, but I fear this has all taken me quite by surprise," said Mrs. Kingsley. "Would you please sit—"

"Thank you, but no. I only came to speak my peace." Charity inched towards the door, but Mrs. Kingsley followed after. The lady frowned, and her husband looked equally troubled. Taking another fortifying breath, Charity steeled herself. Apparently, a simple confession would not be enough.

"I know this may be a bit startling, but it is long overdue," said Charity, her gaze drifting anywhere but on the people before her. "I have long been ashamed of the way I acted—" but she paused and amended, "and how I've continued to act towards the both of you. I wish I could lay all the blame on my mother's poor example, but I was so very hurt by Mr. Kingsley's rejection, and I fear that pain evolved into anger. But regardless, it is inexcusable of me to nurse such a grudge for so long."

"Pardon?" Mr. Kingsley's question forced Charity's gaze to him, and she was met by two brows hovering high up his forehead.

"I rejected you?" he clarified.

"Yes, of course. Everyone was convinced you would offer for me, and then you ran off and married a stranger instead, leaving me marked—"

"I beg to differ, but I never had any intentions to woo you. I certainly never gave any reason for people to think we were courting," said Mr. Kingsley, his gaze bouncing between his wife and her. His eyes were so wide, and his mouth gaping open like a cod, and though Charity had promised herself to behave appropriately for the occasion, she couldn't help but scowl at him.

"We often were thrown together during parties, and you asked me to dance multiple times. Twice a night on more than one occasion—"

"That cannot be true—" But Mr. Kingsley's words cut short when his wife scoffed. His expression fell, his brows knitting together, and she squeezed his hand.

"Forgive me, dearest, but you are not the best judge of your actions or how they are interpreted by others. From the beginning of my time in Bristow, people have whispered about you choosing me over Miss Baxter." Turning to Charity, Mrs. Kingsley's expression fell, her eyes filling with concern. "I know how easily people judge a lady on her marital status, and I am truly sorry for any pain I might've caused you—however inadvertent. I accept your apology, and I hope you shall grant me the same."

Charity's shoulders dropped, the muscles relaxing for the first time in hours (perhaps days), and she stared at the lady, whose expression was the epitome of contrition, making her words ring true.

"I hardly know what to think," said Mr. Kingsley, drawing both ladies' attention. "But you cannot expect a few little words will undo the heartache you've caused, Miss Baxter. It is well and good that you've had a change of heart, but you and your mother have tormented my wife and our family for so long. I fear Mina is far too quick to forgive."

But that earned him a narrowed look from Mrs. Kingsley, who added an arched brow to that and said in a teasing tone, "I would think that you, of all people, would be grateful for how quickly I can forgive, Simon Kingsley."

That drew a wince, and Mr. Kingsley shifted in place with a sigh. Dropping his head, he studied his feet for a few moments before raising his gaze to meet Charity's, all sense of irritation fading away as he said, "If this is the time for apologies, then I suppose I ought to add mine to the mix. I never meant to raise your expectations and always believed it was your family who had given rise to such rumors—not my behavior. I am sorry for my carelessness. Doubly so, for I am well aware of how such a dismissal might've damaged your reputation. I never intended it, and I hope you can forgive me."

Charity stiffened as he spoke, her eyes growing alarmingly misty as the words she'd longed to hear echoed in her ears. Of course, they weren't accompanied by the groveling she'd often imagined, but then, she'd never truly thought Mr. Kingsley's declaration would drift from the realm of fantasy into reality. Her heart groaned as something released inside her, relieving a pressure she hadn't realized was there until it was gone, and it could beat properly once more.

Her eyes fluttered as she tried to stem the ridiculous tears from gathering any more than they had already. Charity Baxter had spent much of her life without blubbering and sobbing like a fool, yet from the offset of the Christmas season, she'd been plagued by such things.

When she was certain she could speak clearly, Charity tried to give a reassuring smile, though it was a little too stiff. "Of course, I accept your apology, Mr. Kingsley. In many ways, I feel I ought to thank you for it. Had I not become a pariah, I would've continued on as I had been, and I shudder to think of what I once was."

But Charity winced and added, "And what I still too often am."

"Oh, we all fall short of what we'd like to be, Miss Baxter," said Mrs. Kingsley with a kindly smile. Then, motioning towards the sofa, she added, "Please, might we not sit and talk a while?"

Charity wanted to say yes. Longed to embrace a new ally and possible friend. But days of fretful thinking had culminated in an ending far happier than she'd imagined, and her heart was filled to bursting. Even now, it thumped happily away, giving her all sorts of fluttery feelings that threatened to draw forth more tears. Another few minutes, and she was bound to make a fool of herself.

"That is kind of you, but I fear I must go," she said with a shake of her head, moving towards the door. Pausing on the threshold, Charity turned and said with a tentative smile, "Perhaps I might call on you another day?"

Mrs. Kingsley grinned, her whole expression lightening as she nodded. "I would love that."

Charity gave another jerky nod, pinching her lips tight together lest she say something to undo the goodwill she'd garnered. But just as her slippered feet hit the hall, she recalled one other detail that needed mentioning.

Spinning in place, she faced them with a grimace. "And I

may have been the one to spread the rumors that you were insolvent to explain why you married Mrs. Kingsley in such a hurried fashion. Thankfully, my pathetic attempt at sabotage did not take. I assure you the only reason I did it was to save my reputation—not that it did any good." But Charity paused and waved that away. "And not that I wish to make excuses for my behavior."

The Kingsleys merely stood there, looking no more surprised than before, and Charity gave another quick bob.

"Cheers," she said, hurrying back the way she'd come.

Chapter 17

"Are you going to sulk for the rest of your visit?"

Thomas refused to acknowledge Ashbrook's question, just as he had every other time the fellow had broached the subject since the Nelsons' Twelfth Night party. As his host, Thomas could hardly avoid him entirely, but he could pretend he hadn't heard Ashbrook.

Turning his gaze to the winter scene, Thomas tried to lose himself in the beauty of Bristow. The walk from the dower house to Avebury Park was hardly long, but the route was circuitous enough to give the impression that it was quite remote and secluded. Trees arched overhead, and he pictured how lovely it would be in the spring when they were covered in blossoms of white and pink. At present, they were laden with snow, which only served to remind him of a certain lady who was quite skilled at using them as weapons in snow battles.

Frowning, Thomas turned his gaze from them and stared down at his feet. Better.

"I have a listening ear," said Ashbrook. "Two, in fact."

His friend lapsed into silence again, but Thomas felt the fellow's attention still fixed on him. Vapor swirled about him as he sighed and turned his gaze down the path. Mrs. Ashbrook and

Phillip walked hand-in-hand, though Thomas suspected it was more from necessity than affection as the boy kept tugging at his mother's hold, yanking her toward the unblemished stretch of snow to their right.

"It might help to unburden yourself," said Ashbrook.

"There is nothing to unburden."

"But—"

"Let it be!"

His friend's brows rose at the sharp tone, and Thomas stopped in his tracks, his head dropping low with a sigh.

"I apologize, Ashbrook. I haven't been myself of late."

"Does it have anything to do with Miss Baxter?"

Thomas's head snapped up, and he scowled. "Certainly not. That's preposterous!"

The answer was so immediate and sharp that he couldn't help but wince. Another heavy sigh swirled in the chill air around him, as he let his shoulders drop.

"I do not mean to be testy with you, Ashbrook. I haven't slept well of late."

That was true enough, for Thomas had hardly slept a wink in the past sennight. Ashbrook nodded, but the fellow's gaze was filled with disbelief. Shaking it away, Thomas quickened his pace to catch up with the others, leaving his friend to follow after.

"Can we go riding today, Mama?" asked Phillip. "Buttercup misses me terribly if I do not visit her regularly."

"Ah, is that so?" she replied, sending her husband a smile over her shoulder. "I'm afraid it is too cold to do so, but we shall visit cousins instead. Aunt Mina and Uncle Simon have promised that Oliver and Lily will be awake. I understand that he has some new soldiers to show you."

Phillip tugged at his mother, dragging her along the path and fairly hopping in his excitement to reach their destination. The child chattered on about all the battles waged, and the strategies one must employ when the enemy's sister tended to toddle through the middle of the battlefield.

With his parents' attention occupied with the lad, Thomas was left to his own devices. But he couldn't decide if that was better or worse than being pestered by Ashbrook, for his mind drifted once more to the lady Ashbrook wished to discuss. His insides twisted as his cruel words rang in his ears and Miss Baxter's expression flashed in his mind's eye. As much as Thomas wanted to believe it had been merely a heated moment, his attack had been too direct and pointed.

But it had been necessary. Deserved, even.

Thomas's footsteps slowed, the distance between him and the others growing as he studied the tips of his boots. If he was so certain of his behavior, why did he need to convince himself again and again? He had two and thirty years to his name, and he knew well enough that justification was the sign of a guilty conscience—and Thomas had been doing little else since his argument with Miss Baxter.

Frowning, Thomas's gaze traced the paths the Ashbrooks made in the snow, and he wondered what Miss Baxter would say at this very moment. No doubt, she would lecture him in that tart tone of hers. As much as he disliked being the object of her fury, Thomas enjoyed seeing her in a passion; she reminded him of an avenging angel, fighting to set the world to rights once more.

Thomas couldn't help but grin at the memory of her embracing the levity of the moment as they'd strutted around the party as Miss Frumpish and Sir Hard-to-Please. Though her wit emerged infrequently, it was there, and when it did, it struck with more force than the endless jests he constantly spouted. To say nothing of the fact that her company was desirable with meandering conversations that had no discernible route as they drifted from one subject to another.

Miss Baxter had confided in him as no one did, entrusting him with truths she'd given to no one else. Making her laugh was a thrill, but gaining that trust was humbling. And oddly empowering. And with a few words, he'd betrayed her. Thomas Callaghan was no saint, and heaven knew he was as flawed as any, but knowing that he'd treated her in such a shabby fashion made his insides squirm, tying themselves into knots.

Why had he done that? As much as he tried to justify it, no answer gave him rest. The memory of Miss Baxter's burning with hurt settled heavy on him, pressing down on him.

"A gift and a word of apology will do the trick," murmured Ashbrook with a hint of a smile in his tone.

Thomas frowned, casting his friend a sideways glance. For all that it might be sound advice at other times, he doubted it would be enough to atone for his sins. Ashbrook watched him from the corner of his eye, with far too much understanding and curiosity, and Thomas tugged at the scarf at his neck, loosening the knot and retying it.

"Have you decided on whether or not you'll accept the publisher's offer?"

Ashbrook's brows lifted in challenge, but Thomas refused to look at him. Then with a tight smile, the fellow sighed and accepted the distraction.

"I have to admit that writing a travel guide is intriguing. It is not so very different from what I've written about life in the navy, and it would provide us the opportunity to travel." Ashbrook's head drifted from side to side as though considering it anew. "It is not what I had ever envisioned doing, but the idea has merit. And they are popular, appealing to both travelers and the curious."

"Where would you visit first?"

And with that, Ashbrook's attention diverted away from Miss Baxter, which ought to have eased some of the tension in Thomas's chest—if Miss Baxter's voice hadn't popped right into his thoughts. He heard her at his elbow, harping about how he was avoiding the subject and distracting Ashbrook with other matters rather than discussing anything of a tender nature.

But Miss Baxter was wrong. She was. Glancing at Ashbrook, Thomas frowned to himself.

The path turned a corner, and Avebury Park loomed ahead, looking picturesque amongst the winter landscape. However, it wasn't the stately structure that held his attention. It was a familiar blue cloak emerging from the front door.

Miss Baxter lifted her face to the sky as though basking in the muted light of the cloudy afternoon, and she drew in a deep breath. Peace settled around her, drawing close like her winter cloak as the tension drained away. Though Thomas had not known her long, he suspected tranquility was a common state for her, though it was quite becoming. Miss Baxter was already quite lovely, and that softness of spirit brought a brightness to her countenance that no amount of rouge could mimic.

Then her gaze turned to see them approaching.

Thomas raised a hand in greeting, a grin stretching across his face—and hers vanished. Spinning away, Miss Baxter marched in the opposite direction, heading down the drive towards the road, her shoulders stiff and posture rigid. Thomas moved before he realized he was doing so (and certainly without a plan), but he couldn't let her escape.

"Miss Baxter!"

But she didn't turn. If anything, her feet moved quicker, and she had a good lead on him. Moving into a jog, Thomas gave chase. The distance shortened, and just as he was about to catch her, his feet hit a patch of ice, and though his boots were good for keeping the snow out, they provided little grip. His leg shot forward, propelled by his momentum and the slippery surface, while his left remained firmly anchored in place.

With a jolt, he crashed to the ground, his elbow and hip taking the brunt of the force, and Thomas was certain something ripped. His muscles felt as though they'd been torn to shreds, and while he lay there waiting for his body to stop throbbing, Miss Baxter was making a hasty retreat.

Groaning, he rolled over to get to his knees, and his right ankle screamed as he tried to get it under him. Then his legs didn't want to cooperate. But he was master here—not them. Focusing on the lady evading him, Thomas shoved aside the aches and pains and rose, unsteadily, to his feet. Then hobbled after her.

So much for his pride.

"Miss Baxter, please." Thomas tried to hurry forward, but his body refused to work as it ought, and he struggled to match her pace, let alone catch her. Only when Avebury Park and the Ashbrooks were well out of sight, and they were closer to her family's home than his friend's, did Thomas finally gain the distance.

"I apologize, Miss Baxter," he said when he was close enough that he didn't have to shout.

But still, she did not slow or acknowledge him.

"Please allow me to make amends."

If anything, Miss Baxter's posture stiffened further, her head rising a fraction. Thomas's abused body began to falter from the bruising pace she'd set, and he struggled for anything that might make her stop and listen.

"I am ashamed of what I said to you, but I give you my word, I didn't mean it. If I could undo the past, I would. I know you've said plenty of things you regret, Miss Baxter. Surely, you understand!"

She stopped, though she did not turn to look at him nor did those rigid shoulders relax. However, Miss Baxter remained in place long enough for Thomas to catch up. When he finally stood before her, the wariness in her gaze made his insides twist anew.

"I do understand, Lieutenant Callaghan," she said in a low voice. Though Miss Baxter stood with that resolute posture, her gaze was trained on the ground. "I know what it is to regret my words, and I am grateful for those who are willing to accept my apologies and forgive."

Thomas hardly dared to smile, but his heart lifted as she spoke, the tension in his chest easing enough so that he could breathe again.

But before he could say a word, she continued, "I once heard it said that forgiveness isn't something one offers another, but it is a gift one gives oneself. Anger and bitterness only hurt oneself, after all. And I may not be perfect at embracing it, but I am trying to be better. I do not wish to hold onto that pain or allow it to fester within me. I wish to be a kinder person, and in that spirit, I forgive you."

The throbbing along the right side of his body was well worth it, and if not for the fact that his limbs refused to work properly, Thomas might've danced a jig right there.

"My deepest thanks, Miss Baxter. My actions have plagued me for days now, and I wish I could properly describe just how much it means to have mended things with you."

That was when her eyes rose to meet his, and Miss Baxter's gaze was cold. "I said I forgive you, Lieutenant Callaghan. I did not say I wish to mend things with you."

And with that, she stepped around him and continued down the lane.

Chapter 18

Gaping, Thomas stared for a long moment before sense returned to him. His joints protested any movement, but he forced them to give chase once more. Thankfully, he caught her quickly.

"I do not understand." Thomas rounded on the lady and planted himself in front of her once more. "If you forgive me, then surely, there is no reason we cannot be friends again."

Miss Baxter showed no flare of temper, looking for all the world as cool as the winter's day, and Thomas's chest tightened once more.

"I've spent too much of my life holding onto hurts, and I refuse to do so anymore. So, yes, I forgive you for everything." Miss Baxter's tone was not like anything he'd heard from her before. Neither haughty, frigid, nor friendly. It was as though she were speaking of the weather to an acquaintance on the street. "However, if you think I can simply forget what happened and wish to be near you again, you are quite mistaken. I have no interest in associating with someone who would purposefully hurt me in such a manner."

"But—"

A quick flash of temper burned in her gaze, silencing him,

but it vanished as Miss Baxter said, "You did not speak in the heat of the moment, sir, so do not pretend otherwise. You were discomforted by the situation and what I was saying, and rather than behaving sensibly and telling me you did not wish to discuss it, you fled. When that did not work, you took my deepest fears and weaknesses and turned them on me. Taunting me. Chastising me. Blaming me. You wished to cause me pain, and you did a good job of it."

"I fully admit I was a cad, and I cannot express how much I regret what I said. I wish I could defend myself, but what can I say? I lashed out and hurt you. It was all my doing—not yours. But please, I do not wish to lose you as a friend."

"Better to be alone than have friends like that, Lieutenant Callaghan."

Stepping around him once more, Miss Baxter continued down the lane, and Thomas stared after her as he sought any response that might refute the charges leveled at him. But no amount of justification could cover those sins, and he would not attempt it. Thomas winced as he hurried after her, his ankle throbbing in time with his rapid heartbeat.

Coming up beside her, he affected a smile and a light tone, "I seem to recall another time when you declared you had no intention of being my friend."

Pausing in place, Miss Baxter stared ahead, not looking at him, despite the jovial expressions he kept trying to give her. Then her eyes turned to him, locking on his gaze with such a determination that Thomas couldn't look away even if he wanted to.

"I cannot be your friend because you have no idea what it means to be one—to me or anyone," she said with a frown. "You wish for me to open my heart up and tell you my troubles, but you refuse to do the same. Friendship requires honesty and trust, and you refuse to embrace either."

Miss Baxter spoke with such finality, and Thomas couldn't think what to say in reply. When he did open his mouth, she merely waved it away.

"What does it matter anyway? You are leaving soon, and our paths shan't cross again." Miss Baxter's voice trembled. It was the slightest show of emotion, but he heard it before she could hide it away. Swallowing, she put on a smile that was as empty as his own had been. "So, continue on your merry way, Lieutenant Callaghan, and do not give me a second thought."

"You forget that I have few other places in England in which to spend my weeks ashore. I am likely to return." However, that excuse sounded weak even to his ears.

Miss Baxter's smile tightened. "As it stands, my parents will either marry me off or leave Bristow. So, I shan't be here when you do."

She turned as though to leave, but paused, her brows drawing together. "You spoke of loneliness as one who truly understands it. I hope one day you can find your way to trusting another, for you are condemning yourself to a solitary life if you insist on keeping everyone at arm's length."

Giving him a curt bob, she added, "Farewell, Lieutenant Callaghan."

And with that, Miss Baxter walked away, leaving Thomas to stare after her. Silently, he pleaded for her to turn around, to return to him, but she never paused as she trudged off into the distance. Not even a single glance behind her. The road carried her around a bend, yet he stood there, uncertain of what to say or do.

Miss Baxter was correct. It wasn't as though they were bound to see each other in the future, so it was of no consequence that they should part ways now. It was disappointing that they would not have the last few weeks together, but what were a few weeks? In the span of a lifetime, they mattered little. There was no future between him and Miss Baxter, so there was no reason to give chase.

When the cold seeped through his boots and clothes, Thomas forced himself to move. His feet wanted to follow after her, but as much as he wished to pester her into speaking with him again, he couldn't deny the truth of her words. Their time had come to an end. Stretching out their farewell served no purpose; better to return to a life without Miss Baxter in it.

Thomas wandered back towards Avebury Park, but he couldn't bear to see anyone, so he continued past it. Pulling his jacket close, he burrowed into his scarf, but a chill had taken hold of him that was far colder than the winter air.

A child cast into the navy was forced to embrace solitude. What did a lad not yet ten years old have to say to a sailor who had offspring older than him? Despite being surrounded by men and hardly allowed any privacy, Thomas had often been left to his thoughts and had learned to enjoy his own company. Yet as he walked along, his mind was as empty as a ship's larder by the end of a voyage.

His feet needed some path to take, so Thomas followed the road as his thoughts fixed on the image of her walking away from him. Never to be seen again. As he had no destination in mind, Thomas was surprised when he crested a hill to find Gladwell House below. There was no point in wandering all over oblivion, so he made his way there. At least the house would be quiet while the Ashbrooks were visiting the Kingsleys. However, when he stepped through the front door, he heard the unmistakable sounds of the family.

How long had he been wandering? But as he had neither pocket watch now nor when he'd set off with the Ashbrooks, Thomas couldn't be certain; it had to be of some duration if they had already concluded their visit to the Park.

Ashbrook poked his head out of the parlor as Thomas divulged himself of his jacket and gloves and hung them on the pegs by the cottage door. "Where have you been?"

"Walking," he murmured as he followed Ashbrook into the parlor to find Mrs. Ashbrook reading while Phillip played with his toys.

"With Miss Baxter, no doubt," she said, glancing at him from over the top of her novel. "I do not care what Mina and Simon say, I do not trust that woman one bit."

Thomas groaned as he finally sat, his body protesting the

abuse it had taken this afternoon, though it was nothing compared to the beating his heart had received. "What do you mean?"

Tucking her finger between the pages, Mrs. Ashbrook shut her book. "Didn't Miss Baxter tell you why she was visiting Avebury Park?"

In all the excitement of seeing her, Thomas hadn't considered how odd it was to see her at the Kingsleys' home.

Mrs. Ashbrook gave a vague wave and opened her book once more. "She called on them suddenly, offering up spice cake and apologies, wishing to make amends."

Thomas's brows rose, and for the first time since that wretched Twelfth Night party, a genuine smile graced his lips. Despite everything, his heart flushed with pride at her courage in doing so. "She did?"

But Mrs. Ashbrook shrugged and returned to her book. "People love to claim redemption and changes of heart when they are sorrowful, but when their resolve is tested, they crumble. I shan't believe it until I see hard evidence through her actions."

"Miss Baxter may be flawed, but she is genuine," replied Thomas. "She truly wishes to be better."

"They all are genuine in the moment," replied Mrs. Ashbrook.

"She is not like that." Thomas's sharp tone drew all the Ashbrooks' gazes to him, all raised brows and wide eyes. But it was his friend who spoke first.

"I think I need to speak with Thomas for a bit."

Rising to his feet, Ashbrook pressed a quick kiss to his wife's head and nodded for Thomas to follow him, and the pair took the stairs and ensconced themselves in the study. Books lay open on Ashbrook's desk with bits of his latest manuscript scattered around it. Several quills were strewn across it all with the remnants of the sharpened tips littering the free places. Ignoring the mess, Ashbrook motioned for the armchairs by the fireplace and sat, steepling his fingers as he studied Thomas.

"You are behaving quite strangely," said Ashbrook with a tone that was far too knowing for Thomas's well-being.

"I apologize for snipping at your wife. I haven't been sleeping well."

Ashbrook's brows rose at that. "Are you blaming your foul mood on exhaustion? I've seen you near dead on your feet, and never once did it make you snap at others."

"Am I not allowed to be out of sorts?" Thomas crossed his arms and sank lower into the armchair. It made him look like a petulant child, but he didn't care.

Leaning forward, Ashbrook studied him for a long moment. "Actually, I am glad to see it. I wish you were out of sorts more often."

Thomas huffed. "That is an odd thing to say to a friend."

"It is an honest thing, which is precisely what one ought to say to a friend."

Those words pricked at his heart, bringing with them Miss Baxter's chastisements, which were close enough to Ashbrook's that Thomas shifted in his seat and frowned.

"I learned long ago not to press the issue, but I want you to know I am always willing to listen, should you need it. Even the most solitary of creatures need a confidant," said Ashbrook.

Solitary creature? Thomas's brows furrowed as he considered that. He'd never thought of himself as such, but even if he had been able to ignore Miss Baxter's assertions, hearing the echo of them from Ashbrook was impossible to overlook.

"I received some troubling news, that is all," said Thomas.

"About Miss Baxter?"

Thomas let his head fall back against the armchair. There were so many things troubling him about her—none of which he wanted to discuss. But there was one bit that kept picking at him. "Her parents are determined to see her married off to Mr. Honeyfield. I cannot bear to think of my friend being tied to such a man. It is a wretched future."

Ashbrook grimaced. "He is an admirer of my work and sought me out at church. I spoke to the man for only five minutes, and it was five minutes too long. I do not envy any lady having to suffer his company."

Shifting in place, Thomas tried to get a comfortable position, but the chair was so decidedly pokey and unpleasant. It didn't help matters that the fire had burned low. Standing, he reached for the wood stacked neatly beside it and added a log.

"It pains me to see her forced into such a dreadful position," said Thomas.

"So, you would be perfectly content if Miss Baxter found a young, amiable man to marry?"

Ashbrook's question struck Thomas, and he jerked around to stare at his friend. His lips almost formed an affirmative, for that seemed the proper answer to give, but his stomach soured at the thought of speaking it. Not that he needed to, for Ashbrook watched him with knowing eyes as Thomas dropped back into his seat.

"Do you really think me a solitary creature?" asked Thomas.

"That isn't what I said."

"You implied it."

Ashbrook considered that, and the moment of silence stretched out for too long. "I suppose I did."

"And?" pressed Thomas.

"Yes, you are a solitary creature." Ashbrook didn't bother offering up honeyed words or rambling explanations, merely laying out the truth in that one word.

Thomas took that and blended it with what Miss Baxter had said as well, sprinkling in his own thoughts and mulling it as thoroughly as the wines that had graced the holiday table.

"Miss Baxter said I keep people at arm's length," murmured Thomas, his head falling back against the chair once more. His gaze fixed on the ceiling, tracing the faint lines of the plaster.

"Did she?"

"Right before she told me she didn't wish to be friends with someone who refuses to be honest with her."

"Did she?" Ashbrook repeated, his tone holding more than a touch of surprise at that.

Thomas wished he could simply wave aside all her concerns, but the fact that he felt more inclined to make a jest at that moment only served to prove the point. He scratched at his forearms, though it did nothing to alleviate the itch, and his lips kept trying to turn up into a silly grin, as though that might hide the truth while Ashbrook watched him with such knowing eyes.

Taking in a deep breath, Thomas forced himself to speak. "I've grown far too used to acting as though nothing is wrong..."

His throat tightened, and instincts nearly had him laughing at himself, the urge to spout some nonsense nearly stronger than his control. But then he imagined Miss Baxter's scowl, and her voice rang in his thoughts, telling him not to be so ridiculous. A faint but genuine smile tugged at the corner of his lips.

"Pretending doesn't seem to be working," murmured Ashbrook.

Straightening, Thomas turned to his friend. This man, who had been with him through so many times, who had never given him any reason to doubt him. Thomas's chest burned as the truth of Miss Baxter's words came back to him. He was a terrible friend, and Ashbrook deserved better.

Taking in a deep breath, Thomas forced himself to meet Graham Ashbrook's gaze. "Might I borrow one of those listening ears you've been bragging about?"

"Thomas, you may have both of them."

Chapter 19

Though handsome features and a ready wit may grant one access to a greater swath of society, Lieutenant Thomas Callaghan had not the prestige of a captain nor a vast array of heroic tales to his name, thus he earned few invitations into the high echelons of society. Where the soldiers often held back a uniform for important occasions, for those at sea, the opportunity to mix in company cropped up so rarely that there was little point.

Thomas had revived his uniform enough to grace Bristow's Christmas festivities, but now, his eyes saw all the smudges of dirt that wouldn't quite come clean. Thankfully, the majority of the jacket was a deep blue, which hid a multitude of marks, but why could they not choose black for the rest of it? Yes, when pristine, the white waistcoat was a stark contrast that caught the eye, but it was deucedly difficult to keep clean.

With his bicorn hat tucked under his arm, Thomas stood before his mirror and turned this way and that, smoothing out the wrinkles, though the maid's iron had erased the lot of them.

"You can stare at yourself all day, and it shan't alter the image one bit," said Graham, leaning against the doorframe with his arms crossed and an irritating smile on his lips.

"It would hardly do to show up looking like a shag-bag. I have much to atone for and little to offer. The least I can do is look dashing and handsome." Turning his gaze back to himself, Thomas frowned and tried to ignore the tightness in his chest. "Perhaps she will simply swoon straight into my arms."

"That is the hope," murmured Graham with a hint of humor in his tone.

Thomas owed Miss Baxter yet another apology: having others mock when you are agitated was not amusing in the slightest.

Mrs. Ashbrook was passing in the hall and paused at her husband's comment, examining the fellow with an arched brow. "Is it?"

Thomas pretended not to notice, but he couldn't help but see his friend wink at his wife, taking her hand in his and raising it to his lips. It was a simple little token, yet Thomas felt as though he were intruding on an intimate moment between husband and wife. Graham spoke in a voice too soft for Thomas to catch, but the words set Mrs. Ashbrook blushing.

Clearing his throat, Thomas drew their attention away from each other before things grew too heated. But Graham looked unrepentant, merely giving his friend a broad smile and a challenging raise of his brows. Yes, Thomas was jealous, but there was no need to rub his nose in it.

"Are you certain about this?" asked Mrs. Ashbrook, though the question was spoken without the usual hard quality that she often employed when speaking about anything or anyone connected to the Baxters. "I know everyone is keen to forgive, but I cannot help but worry it might be a mistake. Please, be cautious."

But if her words were meant to warn, they only strengthen his resolve. Thomas's heart burned as he considered it, and every instinct he possessed told him Mrs. Ashbrook's assessment was incorrect.

Turning to face Mrs. Ashbrook, Thomas bowed in acknowledgment. "I appreciate your concern, but Miss Baxter is not who you think she is. Her heart is far bigger and kinder than people realize."

Mrs. Ashbrook nodded and went on her way while Graham's gaze followed after her. Thomas's chest burned at the sight of his friend's love, written in every inch of his expression. Did he dare hope for such a thing? Frowning, his guilt dredged up his many offenses once more, but Thomas refused to bow beneath the weight of them. He could do this. He would.

"Wish me luck," he said as he strode past his friend.

...

Staring at the parlor wall was not a productive use of her time, but Charity had little other recourse. Mama was off on visits, leaving her alone, which was both a blessing and a curse. Though it meant she'd avoided accompanying her mother on a mission to spread her gossip abroad, it left Charity with little to occupy her time. A stack of abandoned magazines sat on the table beside the sofa, and though she glanced at them once more (as though the titles had somehow altered since she'd tossed them there), none could distract her.

If anything, they only forced her thoughts back to subjects that were best left alone.

Like her mama, Charity was not an accomplished lady. Her art was middling. Her skill with music was even worse. Her needlepoint was adequate but lacked any creative merit. The only thing the Baxter ladies possessed was a sharp tongue and a commanding personality, both of which were of no use to Charity anymore. Leaving her with little else to do.

She might've gone riding if Papa hadn't emptied their stables, ridding themselves even of Mama's beloved gig (one might've thought he'd sold her into slavery for all the wailing and gnashing of teeth that had followed that decision). However, a walk was entirely out of the question, for it would do nothing to keep her thoughts focused on safe subjects.

Charity Baxter was a useless creature.

Frowning at herself, she rose from her chair and walked to the window. Such morose thoughts were entirely unhelpful. Besides, one cannot expect everything to alter in one quick moment. Perhaps with Mrs. Kingsley's aid, she might engage in charity work that truly helped the needy and better lived up to her namesake. Or she might join the lady's literary society. That might be something—

A knock at the door had Charity whirling around as she called out to the servant.

Their manservant opened the door and bowed. "Visitor to see you, miss."

"Oh, thank goodness," she said with a sigh. "Please, bring them in."

Charity didn't know who it was, but it didn't matter. Anyone was better than being left to her own devices at present.

"Good afternoon, Miss Baxter," said Miss Ingalls.

Staring at the young lady, Charity's thoughts emptied altogether, leaving her standing like a wide-eyed statue. Shaking herself free of her stupor, she motioned for the sofa. "Please come in, Miss Ingalls."

The lady stood stiffly for a heartbeat before accepting, her back as rigid as iron as she fiddled with the reticule lying on her lap. Silence dragged out, for Charity couldn't think what to say and had not the slightest idea why Miss Ingalls was calling on her. Their last interlude certainly hadn't hinted at a friendly visit in their future.

Miss Ingalls shifted in her seat. "Miss Baxter..."

But her words drifted off, as she stared at her hands.

"I—" Miss Ingalls stopped once more and took a deep breath. Closing her eyes, she held it for a few seconds before releasing it and saying in a rush, "I owe you an apology for my behavior at the Nelsons' party. The secret you shared during the game took me by surprise—"

But the lady paused and shook her head. "That is no excuse.

The truth is that while I was taken aback, I was unwilling to accept your remorse. You have caused me great pain, and I saw an opportunity to give some of that back."

Miss Ingalls huffed. "What little good it did. I am thoroughly ashamed of how I acted and what I said, and I hope you can forgive me."

Charity straightened. "Certainly."

"I—" Miss Ingalls paused and finally met her gaze. "Pardon?"

"I forgive you fully and unabashedly," said Charity, leaning forward as though that might further emphasize that truth. "I have developed a newfound love of forgiveness, and as I require it from you, I cannot withhold it."

Brows creeping upward, Miss Ingalls held her gaze for several quiet moments. "You truly meant what you said that night, didn't you?"

"I have been raised to believe myself superior to everyone, only to discover how wrong I am." Charity sighed, her shoulders lowering. "I couldn't understand how painful derision and mockery is until I was on the receiving end of it, and even then, it took years for me to comprehend how much damage it does."

Pausing, Charity forced herself to speak, though her voice wobbled. "And how much damage I have done. I ought to have admitted my guilt sooner or in private, but I fear I was too cowardly."

Silence fell, but Charity could not raise her gaze from her lap as so many other memories assaulted her mind, bringing with it so many others who deserved similar apologies. Perhaps she ought to do more of it; that would certainly be a more worthy use of her time than sitting about, staring out parlor windows.

"I have always admired your confidence and fortitude," said Miss Ingalls, though she hesitated before adding, "I suppose I ought to say I was jealous of it."

"And I suppose I ought to admit that much of it was playacting," replied Charity with a rueful grin. "Like predators, society thinks weakness makes you prey. You cannot allow them to see you quaking in your slippers."

Miss Ingalls' grin matched Charity's. "Then I am doubly jealous of your acting skills."

The silence returned for a long moment, and though neither looked directly at the other, they exchanged glances while Charity attempted to gather the courage Miss Ingalls had praised; her heart was already raw for having exposed so much of it of late, but she couldn't bear to see the lady leave.

Hiding the fretful energy that would have her fidgeting, Charity forced the question out, "Would you care for some tea?"

Miss Ingalls beamed at her. "Yes, please."

The bell was rung, the refreshments sent for, and the pair settled in for a good coze. Or as good as one could get between former enemies now seeking common ground. Stilted questions came at first—the same uninspired queries that dotted most shallow conversations—but from there, they delved into different areas, and Charity was quite surprised to see how many opinions they shared. While dissimilar in so many fashions, they shared more interests than Charity had expected.

Perhaps Miss Ingalls might become a friend.

In all honesty, Charity couldn't say if she'd ever had one among her peers. Even before her descent into disgrace, those closest to her had been subordinates, there to do her bidding, rather than true companions and confidants, and Miss Ingalls hadn't even been that, falling too often into the role of victim—

A knock at the door drew Charity's thoughts short, and she turned to see the manservant enter once more with a low bow.

"Lieutenant Callaghan is here to see you, miss. Should I show him up?"

Charity stopped breathing as she stared at John. Her traitorous little heart wanted to order Lieutenant Callaghan brought posthaste, but there was no good to be had in it. Whatever he was or might've been to her, Lieutenant Callaghan was a sailor leaving their shores soon, never to be seen again. "That way lies madness," as the Bard once wrote, and though *King*

Lear was a travesty of a story, that line was rife with wisdom.

"No, John. Send him away." Charity's stomach twisted, but she ignored it and turned back to Miss Ingalls, pasting on a smile. But the lady was watching her with raised brows.

"Have you two quarreled?" she asked once the servant was gone, and the door shut.

"You speak as though we are more than acquaintances, but I assure you I have not laid eyes on the gentleman before his arrival a month ago." And then Charity added with a smile, "I am merely occupied with a far more interesting conversation and do not wish for him to interrupt."

Miss Ingalls' brows shot upward, her eyes narrowing. "Anyone with sense can see there is something more than a passing acquaintance between you. Not only did I see the pair of you together on New Year's, but I have heard plenty of rumors that you are often in company together—both during the festivities and around town. What has happened?"

Lips pinched together, Charity considered that. Though some part of her wished to keep it secret, a greater part of her longed to give the thing a voice; it had been bottled up in her thoughts, and no amount of thinking it through would give the same relief as spilling the whole sordid affair. And no one else wished to hear the tale.

So Charity spoke, laying out the whole confusing business from beginning to end, sparing not a single detail, even including those wonderful moments when she'd hoped for a happier outcome. And Miss Ingalls proved herself a fine friend when she gasped at the wretched parts and offered up more than a few epitaphs impugning Lieutenant Callaghan's honor upon hearing the worst of it.

"And now, he has arrived on your doorstep, and you sent him away?" asked Miss Ingalls.

Charity frowned. "And what ought I to do? Welcome him with open arms? The man does not want to be my friend. He wants a plaything. Someone to tease and twit until he sails away, never to be seen again. If nothing else, I need to protect my heart from becoming more invested, for the silly thing doesn't seem to realize he cannot be trusted with it."

Miss Ingalls let out a low noise, almost a hum but with a pensive quality to it, her brows pinching together. "I wouldn't have thought you capable of being a good friend, yet now, I am quite intrigued by the possibility. However, I am afraid of you as well. Ought I to give up when I have the opportunity to gain another ally simply because my feelings might be at risk?"

Though it was entirely unnecessary, Charity shook her head, which Miss Ingalls accepted with a smile before continuing.

"You cannot gain love without risk. He may prove himself false, or he may simply be a flawed man attempting to be better. He may disappear from your life, never to be seen again, or he may wish never to be parted. Lieutenant Callaghan may be precisely what you long for, but you cannot know for certain before you have the opportunity to truly know him."

Gaze dropping, something in her seemed to deflate, though Miss Ingalls' posture remained as proper as before. "Do not leap in carelessly, Miss Baxter, but do not throw aside possibilities with reckless abandon, either. Make him earn your trust and affection again, but do not let go unless you are certain he is unworthy."

Charity shifted in her seat and sighed. "You are making too much sense for my good, Miss Ingalls. I fear it would be far easier to cut him off."

"Regrets are far harder to bear than crushed hopes. The latter hurts more in the beginning, but those wounds heal eventually. The former's pains fester, growing stronger with each year," she said with a weak smile.

Frowning, Charity leaned forward and studied the young lady. But Miss Ingalls straightened and rose to her feet.

"I'm afraid the time is getting away from me," she said as she straightened her skirts.

Heart sinking, Charity nodded as she couldn't think of a valid reason to keep Miss Ingalls there any longer, but she led the young lady to the front door herself.

"I am glad we had the opportunity to speak today," said Miss Ingalls, as she paused in the entryway.

Charity swallowed past the lump in her throat and nodded. "Might I call on you sometime?"

For half a heartbeat, the weight of the world pressed down on her, threatening to crush her while Miss Ingalls paused. "I would enjoy that."

Charity's heart lightened, and she took a deep breath with another sharp nod. Then with a few words of farewell, she opened the front door, and Miss Ingalls stepped out into the afternoon sun. And they both froze at the sight of Lieutenant Callaghan seated on the front steps.

"Miss Baxter." The man popped up from his cold perch and spun to face her. Giving Miss Ingalls a vague nod, he stepped forward. "Please, might I have a moment of your time?"

Gaze darting between the gentleman and Miss Ingalls, Charity didn't know what to do. The fellow's gaze pleaded for her to accept, and her new friend gave her a beaming smile, making it clear what she thought Charity ought to do. But her heart stuttered in her chest, warning her of what might happen.

"Do come in, Lieutenant Callaghan." Had she spoken those words? With Miss Ingalls close to laughing, Charity wasn't certain it had been herself, but neither did she stop the fellow from stepping across the threshold. Miss Ingalls gave them another bright farewell, though neither Charity nor Lieutenant Callaghan responded as they shut the door behind him.

John poked his head out from the cupboard where he was polishing the silver and hurried to take the visitor's things before she led Lieutenant Callaghan into the parlor. Stiff as a board, Charity forced her knees to bend and sat on the sofa, motioning for him to do the same, though he shook the offer away. Standing there with his hands tucked behind him, he looked more like he was reporting to a superior officer than a friend, and there was an air about him that felt like a beast waiting to break free of its cage.

Good heavens, he was a sight to behold. Charity didn't ascribe to the obsession many women had for men in uniform, but at present, she saw the appeal. Of course, Lieutenant Callaghan usually looked more liable to burst into laughter than fight to the death, and it was difficult to treat a jester seriously—no matter his clothing.

"I tried to think of something to bring," he finally said. "Some gift or treat that might soften your heart. But I did not think there is a large enough cake or biscuit."

At any other time, such a statement would've been accompanied by a glint of humor in his eyes or a quirk of a smile on his lips, but Lieutenant Callaghan merely stood there, at the ready, his gaze holding hers.

"And I realized it is not sugar and fat that I need to bring—just the truth."

Charity perked at his statement, her brows raising as he continued on.

"Though many know bits and pieces, I have never told anyone the whole of the story. Not even my closest friends. However, I want to give this to you because you are right. I hide in plain sight, lying and pretending rather than letting anyone near."

Lieutenant Callaghan's throat bobbed, but his gaze never wavered. "I was engaged."

Chapter 20

Puffing out his cheeks, Thomas let out a breath and studied the toes of his boots. Plans were well and good but following through with them was another thing altogether. For all that he'd practiced this speech, having her lovely eyes trained on him ate away at his composure.

"Oh." The sound gave little away, other than Miss Baxter's surprise, and Thomas refused to think much about it. Regardless of what came next, he needed to tell her the whole of it.

"I met Miss Patience Berry while I was ashore for some months. Our ship needed vast repairs, and we were cut loose for some time with nothing to do." In a rush, the memory of her face came to him, that first moment they'd met in the street, her expression all bright and flirtatious as he'd helped her with the packages she'd "dropped."

Inching backward, he slumped onto a chair. "We were swept up in a grand romance, full of bouquets, poetry, and lingering looks. When I proposed, I hardly expected her to accept as my prospects were so few. I do not think I can ever describe the thrill of the moment when she agreed to be my wife. It was like seeing a sunrise for the first time, the light casting the world in all new hues."

Thomas stopped and straightened as he realized to whom he was speaking. Perhaps it was not the wisest thing to divulge to the lady he wished to court, but when he met her gaze, he found not condemnation or jealousy; Miss Baxter's eyes were warm, a faint smile on her lips.

"I knew you were a romantic," she whispered.

Clearing his throat, Thomas shifted in place and wondered how much more to say. But in for a penny, in for a pound, as they say. Really, it was a silly phrase for there was a vast difference between the two sums, and for a man with little to his name, he could not risk the latter. But that was neither here nor there.

"I wanted to marry her that very day, but her parents rightly insisted I needed more than a midshipman's income before we could start a life together. When I was called back to sea, I threw myself into my lieutenant's exam, studying as though the devil himself would steal away my soul if I failed. I refused to allow our future to follow that of my parents, scrimping by with hardly a farthing to my name."

Thomas sighed as he tried to find the proper words for it all. He had relived those years so many times in his head, but it was quite different from describing all those long hours, pouring over books. The long stretches while he waited desperately for her letters, filled with comfort and motivation. How much he'd fretted and prayed that the examiners would be merciful.

"In the end, it hardly mattered, for though I gained my rank, there were no positions available. I remained a midshipman for a long while," he said with a frown. "We were engaged for three long, agonizing years. During that time, I saw her as often as I could, sometimes spending the majority of my shore leave traveling to and from her home, and I wrote her religiously. It didn't matter that my letters could only be sent when we reached a place with reliable mail or if we crossed paths with packet ships bound for England, I saved them up and sent off great stacks of letters to her."

His gaze grew unfocused the longer he turned his attention

to the past. "I cannot describe what it was like to see one of those vessels on the horizon, hoping that they bore our post. The longing fills you to bursting, promising you that today you shall be showered in words from your loved one, connecting you with their mundane world. All the while knowing that more often than not, your hope will be dashed."

Letting out a heavy breath, Thomas turned a rueful smile on her. "Forgive me if I am growing maudlin."

But Miss Baxter merely raised her brows at that. "I like seeing your maudlin side. No matter how much you pretend otherwise, it is a part of you."

Thomas huffed, ducking his head with a nod.

"Miss Berry?" prodded Miss Baxter, and the sound of Patience's name on her lips sent a shudder down his spine.

With a scoff, Thomas shook his head. "I thought she was at home, pining for me as I did her. And when her letters slowed, I believed it was merely a stroke of bad luck. Post goes missing all the time, and it isn't uncommon for letters to get waylaid for months. It was disheartening but nothing to fret about. And when I was set ashore in England once more, I didn't care that it cost me a pretty penny to arrive on her doorstep or that the time we'd have together was hardly worth the expense. I simply had to see her."

Miss Baxter stiffened, her brow wrinkling as her gaze seemed to plead with him that what she suspected would not be true. And she was correct in a way.

"My dear Patience was quite surprised to see me, but not as much as I was to find her married and expecting her first child. She claimed she hadn't been unfaithful, but though I may play a fool at times, I am capable of simple arithmetic. My last shore leave had been only eight months prior, so unless she met and married the fellow in a matter of weeks, she must've been courting him before that visit. But even if that were not the case, I think marrying a man while being engaged to another would fulfill even the narrowest definition of 'unfaithful.' However, we agreed to disagree."

Puffing out his cheeks, Thomas let out a hard sigh and frowned. "To add insult to injury, she wanted to 'part as friends.' As though the whole thing were a simple misunderstanding."

A flutter of muslin, and then Miss Baxter was seated in the armchair beside him, her brows all pinched together as she reached for his hand and paused, as though wishing to give him comfort and uncertain about whether or not to do so. Thomas snatched the opportunity and the offered limb, weaving her fingers through his.

"She claimed I was too ardent and demanding with my mountains of missives," he muttered with a frown. "What I thought were love letters, tenderly laying my heart bare to her, were irritants and far too emotional. 'Unappealing' was the word she used. Apparently, I am far more acceptable as a distraction than a proper husband."

Gripped in that memory, Thomas slipped into silence as Patience's voice rang in his memory as fresh as it had been when she'd spoken. While courting, it had seemed melodious, but now, he heard the shrill edge to it.

Only when several long minutes had passed did he venture to look at Miss Baxter, who sat there stiff and rigid, her nostrils flaring as she sucked in deep breaths.

"That little..." Miss Baxter fairly growled as she paused, as though searching for the proper word. "Trollop! That..." Her lips pinched together, her scowl deepening. And when she met Thomas's gaze, her own burned with fury. "I know of quite a few names I'd like to call her, though none of them are appropriate to speak aloud. How dare she! It is one thing to change her mind, but to allow you to discover the truth in such a manner and then lay all the blame on you? She ought to be drawn and quartered!"

Thomas couldn't help the laugh. It slipped out before he knew it was coming, but for all that he'd seen her puffed up in a temper before, it had usually been directed at him and not on his behalf.

"Thank you," he murmured.

But that drew a puzzled look. "For?"

Pausing, Thomas tried to think how to describe it. Then with a shrug, he replied, "For being you."

Miss Baxter looked away, but there was a hint of a smile on her lips before she hid it away. Her hand remained in his, hanging between the two armchairs, and though Thomas knew he ought to release it, he couldn't bring himself to do so.

"Your parents and then the lady you loved," murmured Miss Baxter, her brows furrowing. "It is little wonder you guard yourself when you have been so betrayed by those who ought to cherish you."

Thomas stiffened, his heart thumping a rapid beat as she reached the conclusion he'd been slowly working towards over days, weeks, and even years. Yet she understood without him having to say it. And now, his throat decided to stop working.

Forcing air into his lungs, he pressed forward. "That night at the Nelsons', I did feel something stirring for you, and it frightened me. Everything in my life has taught me not to trust. It is better to keep others at a distance, for if you love someone, they will abandon you."

"Not Mr. Ashbrook. He has been your friend for years and never turned his back on you." The answer came without hesitation, a challenging raise of her brow accompanying it.

Wincing, Thomas nodded. "Yes, I am coming to see the flaws in my logic, Miss Baxter. But it is not easy to see truth amidst pain."

"And that is why you need friends. They help you to see," she replied with a hint of her tart tone, though it was softened by a faint smile.

"Again, I am coming to understand that," Thomas replied with a self-deprecating grin. But it fled as he considered his past behavior. "Unfortunately, not before I caused someone great pain; someone who has grown dear to me, despite insisting she doesn't wish to be my friend on multiple occasions."

Rising from his seat while still maintaining his hold on her hand, Thomas squatted before her, so that he might face her fully. "I may have apologized for what I said, but I never apologized for what was been perhaps my greatest sin."

Sucking in a deep breath, Thomas shook his head. "I have been a poor friend to you, Miss Baxter. I don't know if I would've ever recognized it if not for your..."

"Interference?" she offered with a hint of a smile.

"Guidance." Brushing his thumb along the back of her knuckles, he mulled over his words. His mouth dried, and his heart gave a frantic beat. Though he hoped for a certain answer, Thomas knew she was well within her rights to say no, and the thought of it held his tongue captive for a moment. "I know you've said you do not wish to be friends, but might we try again? I am drawn to you, Miss Baxter, and I cannot let you go without a fight. Please, say I have not lost you."

Bristow was brimming with apologies of late. In the past sennight, Charity had been party to more than she cared to count, and despite the growing frequency of them, she still felt awed upon hearing the words. Of course, it was far better when they were directed at her rather than the other way around.

The arguments she'd laid out for Miss Ingalls had been sound. Logical. Even now, Charity knew it was foolish to open herself up to a man who was bound to leave so soon, yet his words wrapped around her heart like a thick blanket, all cozy and warm. She sat there, staring into his eyes, and despite knowing there might be danger ahead, she couldn't turn away from the path before her.

Charity knew full well how greatly he feared vulnerability. Yet, here he sat, laying bare everything he'd kept hidden. Showing it all to her. There was no gift he could've brought that would've been finer than that.

"I propose a plan," he said.

Charity blinked rapidly, her brows shooting upwards, and Lieutenant Callaghan blushed.

"Not propose, propose. Though I wouldn't say I am opposed to the idea..." Then he leaned back on his heels and winced, his cheeks turning even pinker. And despite the weight of his meaning striking deep into her heart, Charity couldn't help but laugh at the man; she'd never expected to see him flustered.

But her gaze fell to their joined hands, his thumb still tracking patterns along her skin. Lieutenant Callaghan cared for her. Despite having seen the hints of it before and even calling it to his attention, Charity couldn't quite believe it.

"I think we ought to take the time given us. I shall be called away before long, but we have at least a fortnight. We ought to make the most of it. Spend every moment we can together. Come to know one another as we ought."

"But what then?"

Lieutenant Callaghan shrugged. "When I am dragged from your side, we will ply each other with a mountain of missives."

"Even if we could afford the post, my parents wouldn't approve of me writing to a man who is not my intended. And we may move, and what then? And they expect me to marry soon. What of that? I see nothing but troubles."

Raising her hand to his lips, Lieutenant Callaghan closed his eyes and pressed a kiss to her knuckles, savoring that touch as much as she. And when he met her gaze once more, Charity's breath caught as she stared into those bright blue eyes.

"I do not know what the future brings, but we can sort it out if we wish to. I know we can."

Raw and bear, his heart lay before her, ready for Miss Baxter to accept it or crush it. In her eyes, Thomas saw the battle waging, and watched as the tide turned in his direction. The worry still strained at the edge of her lips, and he longed to kiss them away. Once the image had taken hold of his mind, his heart wouldn't let it go. Especially after allowing himself to kiss her hand. Thomas could well picture what embracing Miss Baxter would feel like, but that was too great a liberty to take.

For now.

Turning her hand in his, Thomas held her eyes as he pressed another to her palm. The softness of her skin brushed against his lips, and he poured his heart into his gaze, letting her see the whole of it. He would never hide it away again. Not from her.

"What say you?" he whispered.

"Can I give any answer but yes?" she answered with a hint of a sigh.

"Of course, you can."

But Miss Baxter shook her head. "No, I cannot. I am not ready to let you go."

A smile stretched across his face, and Thomas shot to his feet, pulling her up in one fluid movement. And then she was in his arms, her feet dangling down as he lifted her.

"You shan't regret it," he whispered, his lips brushing her ear. "I give you my word."

"I shall hold you to that."

Setting her down once more, Thomas stood flush against her, and for all that he clung to his gentlemanly decorum, he was unable to step away. Perhaps just a little kiss...Thomas drew closer, longing to feel her lips against his. The briefest hint of her skin—

Thomas stiffened. Miss Baxter deserved better than to be mauled by a desperate man in a rush to steal away her heart. She deserved a proper wooing, and their whole situation was far too rushed as it was. So, he gathered the whole of his self-control and put enough distance between them that he could offer up his arm to her. Then affecting a haughty tone, he looked down his nose at her.

"Might I convince Miss Frumpish to join me on a walk about the grounds? This parlor is ghastly and offends my delicate sensibilities."

"Why, Sir Hard-to-Please, if you think the grounds are any

better, you shall be sorely disappointed," she said with a mock scowl as she took his arm. But then her brows furrowed in earnest as Miss Baxter glanced at him. "Her name was Patience?"

The shift in subjects had Thomas struggling to comprehend, but he nodded, glancing at her with a puzzled frown. "Yes. What of it?"

Miss Baxter smothered a laugh and shook her head. "I see you have a weakness for inappropriately named ladies. Not very patient, was she?"

That drew forth a huff of laughter. "I suppose not."

With eyes sparkling, she led him towards the door, and Thomas couldn't help but stare at her while his heart lightened. Yes, one way or another, they would find a way. Together.

Chapter 21

One Year Later

Between delays on the road and an unusually wet winter, which alternated between rain, sleet, and snow, one could not count on the postman's schedule. Yet knowing he may not have arrived (and there may not even be a letter for her even if he had), Charity couldn't help but appear on Gladwell House's doorstep a mere five minutes after the postman's usual rounds.

Pulling her cloak tighter around her, she stomped her feet in a vain attempt to get some feeling back into her toes and winced as she dumped great clumps of slush on the Ashbrooks' front steps. The manservant opened the door, and Charity swept in, not bothering to divest herself of her things before hurrying into the parlor. Phillip looked up from his place at his mother's feet before turning back to his menagerie of wooden animals.

"Tabby, I apologize for bursting in here unannounced, but I couldn't wait until tonight," she said as the lady rose from her seat and greeted her with a buss. "Has the post arrived?"

As much as Charity knew she ought to at least pretend that

the visit wasn't purely selfish, the hope of a letter made it impossible to equivocate. Tabby Ashbrook attempted to act affronted over the direct question, but it dissolved into a laugh as she reached for the stack of envelopes sitting neatly on the table beside the sofa.

"I know what it feels like to wait anxiously for any word, so I shan't tease you," she said, handing the entire group over. Eyes aglow, Charity sifted through the missives. The inconsistency of the naval mail meant they were subjected to periods of famine and feast, waiting for weeks before a flood arrived in her hand, and today was no exception.

"For all that Lieutenant Callaghan was circumspect in his conversation, he certainly has plenty to say now," said Tabby, eying the dozen envelopes.

Charity glanced between them and the sofa, knowing full well that she ought to spend at least a quarter of an hour chatting before making off with her treasure, but Tabby waved her to the door.

"Away with you, now. I know you are desperate to devour every word."

Leaping forward, Charity swept her up in a quick hug before turning away with a bright, "Thank you!"

Hurrying back to the front door, she paused at the threshold and spied the jacket hanging on a peg. A quick look behind told her the hall was empty, so Charity dug into her reticule and retrieved her last two pennies, then reaching for the jacket pocket—

"Stop that this instant!"

Charity jerked around to see Tabby standing there, hands on her hips.

"I have told you we do not want your money."

With a sigh, Charity returned the coins to her reticule. "But—"

"But nothing. Thomas Callaghan is my husband's closest friend, and we have grown rather fond of you as well," said Tabby, employing that same facetious tone Thomas loved so much, and the reminder panged in Charity's heart; would he never return to their shores? But she jerked back to the conversation at present when Tabby continued, "As neither of you can afford such hefty postal fees at present, and we are experiencing a run of good luck ourselves, we wish to pay for it. There is little else we can do for you two."

Lip pinched tight, Charity longed for something to say or do to convey the way her heart warmed at that generosity. But there was nothing more to do than give her an earnest and hearty, "Thank you."

"Lieutenant Callaghan has become a much better man because of you, so thank you," she said before nodding at the door. "Now, off with you. Go devour your love letters."

Hugging them to her chest, Charity beamed and nodded. But paused when Tabby added, "You are still planning on attending tonight?"

"Certainly. Mama is pestering me to join them at the Thompsons' for their New Year's Eve party, but Papa said I am free to join you instead."

Tabby nodded. "We have nothing grand planned, mind you, but we would love for you to attend."

Something in her tone had Charity staring at the lady, her brow furrowing. "I shall."

"Good," said Tabby with a curt nod. "The Kingsleys are sending a carriage—"

"That isn't necessary," said Charity with wide eyes. "That is far too generous. I can walk like I do whenever I visit."

"But not in an evening gown," said Tabby, shooing her towards the door. "Do not argue. It is already settled. It will be in front of your home at eight."

There was no arguing with the lady when she got that tone of voice, so Charity grinned like a ninny. She hadn't realized how rare such joyful emotions were in her life until Thomas swept in and gave her reason to. Now, she walked about looking every bit the fool she'd accused him of being.

Then Charity stepped out into the world. Though the sky

was gray above, it felt as though the sun warmed her skin. The clouds were not the happy, fluffy sort but a solid wall of dingy white, and with the weather being so fickle that it was spring one moment and winter the next, the path from Gladwell House to her home was hardly picturesque. Yet Charity had a skip in her step.

Clinging to her letters, she longed to tear into them and devour every word, but she'd learned her lesson and waited until she was home, though she spent the entire journey imagining just what Thomas might say. The path to and from had grown so familiar, and Charity's thoughts meandered as her feet led her along.

A new year. With the Christmas season in full swing once more, every evergreen bough, yule log, and carol brought with it memories of Thomas. Not that she needed any reason to remember him, but it was far more pointed as she compared each day to that which had passed last year.

Pausing at the edge of town, Charity gazed over the murky fields and breathed in the winter air. How different her life was now. How much greater. Charity had never known such peace. Contentment was not a word used in the Baxter household; one should never be content with what one has, for there is always something greater that can be coveted—always someone better to tear down. But now she understood what it meant to be happy with one's place in the world.

Giving a sigh that was suitable for a lovesick lady, Charity continued along the lane. As she passed the shops, she nodded at those shopping before the New Year's Eve festivities began. Ladies and gentlemen greeted her in turn, and Charity forced herself not to beam, though her footsteps grew lighter. A proper place in the world, indeed.

Juniper Court drew near, and only the stack of letters in her hand allowed Charity to hold onto her equanimity. Whichever ancestor had chosen the name had chosen poorly. It tripped and rolled along the tongue in a happy manner, but the building looked stodgy and gray. Though perhaps that was a bit overdone, for it looked precisely like all the rest along the street. It had the distinction of being set back from the road with a bit of garden around it that made the house passably pretty in the high summer, but it had an air of melancholy that no amount of daisies, lilies, and roses could overcome.

Charity ducked behind a large tree that blocked her from passing view. Turning towards the wall that surrounded her home, she tucked several of the missives into her bodice, shifting them into place so they drew no attention to their hiding place. And having worn a dress with loose sleeves, she stuffed one right after the other up the length of her arms like stiff little soldiers. Taking one of her hairpins, she secured the last one to her cuff; it wasn't a firm hold, but it would do for now.

She needed a larger reticule. Or a better pocket.

Straightening her cloak to hide her sleeves, Charity walked gingerly towards the front door. Paper scraped against her arms and chest, and she barely breathed as each movement shifted the letters clinging precariously to her person. But she managed to get into the house without any trouble.

Passing the parlor door, she ignored the sounds inside and the stacks of crates piled haphazardly and made her way to the stairs before anyone noticed.

"Charity?"

Pausing on the landing, she turned slowly around to see Mama standing at the bottom of the stairs. "Yes?"

That sounded innocent enough, didn't it?

"Where have you been?"

As Charity saw no reason to lie, she said, "The Ashbrooks."

That earned her no further questions, though Mama's gaze narrowed. "I understand your father has given you permission to dine with them tonight."

"He has." Charity forced herself to breathe, though the hairpin began to slip. Twisting her hand, she grasped the cuff before any of her letters could fall, though her wrist wrenched awkwardly.

Mama's expression pinched, but that was nothing new; her visage always looked a tad sour, but doubly so when gazing at the young lady who dared to reject Mr. Honeyfield's offer of marriage. But the less Charity thought on that score, the better.

With a huff, Mama turned away and dismissed her daughter with a curt wave of her hand. "You ought to go through the attics and make certain everything you wish to keep is packed up properly."

"Of course, Mama." Turning on her heel, Charity climbed the stairs, though her feet felt heavier than before. It would be some weeks before they left Bristow, but what then? With the paper scratching against her skin, Charity was keenly aware of how much she depended on the Ashbrooks' kindness. What would she do without them ferrying her letters?

Granted, her parents were far more likely to welcome Thomas's suit now that the only other viable option had been chased away, but what if they didn't? Charity was old enough that she did not require their permission to marry, but could she do so without their approval? Questions swirled about her thoughts as she made her way to her bedchamber, but just as Charity felt they would overpower her, his voice rose in her thoughts, dispelling them with one simple sentence.

"We will find a way."

Thomas had said some variation of that every time she'd voiced a concern, and as much as she wanted concrete plans in place, it gave her some comfort. They'd managed so far, and as long as he desired her, Charity would not give up without a fight.

Chapter 22

Stepping into her bedchamber, Charity locked the door behind her and hurried to the bed, freeing each letter and dropping it atop the bedclothes. Sitting down, she kicked off her slippers, tucked her feet beneath her, and set about opening each missive and placing them in chronological order.

Tucking herself into her pillows, Charity took the topmost one and began to read.

"My Dearest Love"

Charity sighed. Thomas had a wide selection of endearments he employed; some made her smile, others made her laugh, but this one never failed to make her swoon. Such tender little words.

Losing herself in the descriptions of his life aboard the ship, Charity gorged herself on every word, reading it twice over before moving to the next one. Some were one continuous thought, others were bits and pieces over a week, but each word was precious. Though he would likely laugh at the comparison, Charity thought his letters were as stirring as anything Scott or Byron wrote; Thomas was a poet through and through.

The sunlight traveled the length of the room as she sifted through his letters. They sounded so like the man himself. Affable and joyful, but with a touch of earnestness that had been absent those first weeks of their acquaintance. Charity savored those bits the most as he brought more and more of himself to the forefront, laying each bare for her to see.

And the more he did, the more she loved him.

At the last signature, Charity sighed and leaned her head back against the headboard. These were the best and worst of days, for as wonderful as the reading was, her heart ached the moment it was over. Now, she must wait for weeks—maybe even a month, perhaps two—before she'd hear from him again. Of course, there were her responses to compose. That wasn't as thrilling as receiving, but Charity adored responding directly to the things he'd written. That was as close to a conversation as they wont to have while he was an ocean away.

The clock chimed, and Charity finally noticed how dark the room had grown. Straightening, she counted the chimes, her heart sinking with each one. Good heavens! The hour was growing late.

No matter how she longed to remain precisely where she was and revel in her post, the Ashbrooks expected her tonight, and she could not throw them over now. Especially not after assuring her hostess that she was attending. Besides, Tabby seemed quite eager for her to be there.

Gathering up the letters, Charity placed them in order once more and tucked them into her dressing table drawer to keep them separate from the stacks she'd already responded to. Beside it sat a rolled-up paper, which she straightened to gaze upon the profile she'd drawn of Mr. Hard-to-Please. Smiling at the silliness, she then it over to see the genuine one she'd completed on the back. Kissing her fingertips, she pressed them to Thomas's lips and returned the paper to its hiding place.

Charity rose and stood before her wardrobe, examining her scant options for the evening when a thought struck her.

Tabby had been more than merely eager for her tonight. Determined more like. The past year had seen many changes in Charity's life, and though her standing with the Ashbrooks and Kingsleys was now amicable, she wouldn't call Tabby a confidant. A friend, to be certain, but not with the closeness that had them desperate for each other's company.

Was something afoot?

Charity tried to banish it from her thoughts as she dressed in her finest gown (which flattered her figure and eyes to perfection) and while she spent an inordinate amount of time arranging her coiffure. Her looks didn't matter in the slightest for this was simply a party amongst friends, not some elaborate plan to surprise her. Thomas was still aboard his ship—not in Bristow.

Of course, it was like him to do such a thing.

But Tabby's strongly worded invitation signified nothing; Thomas was not going to attend the Ashbrooks' New Year's Eve party. And spending a few extra minutes on her toilette was only right and proper. She was a guest of the Ashbrooks, and she ought to look her best. That was all.

Her insides fluttered as she stared at her reflection, and those thoughts followed her as she put on her cloak and climbed inside the Kingsleys' carriage. And still, Charity's thoughts returned to impossible things. No matter how much she tried to be reasonable, her heart dredged up the image of Thomas standing in the Ashbrooks' parlor, all pleased with himself for having orchestrated the surprise.

Beginning the New Year together.

Fidgeting with her cloak, Charity tried to focus on the passing landscape. Lanterns hung from the houses on either side of the street, the lights glimmering as they passed. But her heartbeat was too quick to ignore. He was coming. He was. Surely, it was so.

Charity flew from the carriage the moment it stopped and fairly danced on her toes as she waited for the Ashbrooks to answer her knock. She was greeted with warm words and smiles and led into the parlor. The world slowed, and Charity's breath caught as she stepped through the doorway, her eyes bright as she searched the party.

Thomas wasn't there.

Charity's smile remained in place, but only by summoning all her strength and wrapping it around her heart; it wasn't the Ashbrooks' fault that she'd allowed her hopes to run away with her. The Kingsleys came forward and greeted her, along with the other guests, and Charity held fast to her equanimity, trying to be gratuitous. Apparently, Tabby simply longed to have her at their party.

That was something to celebrate, wasn't it?

The evening continued as such evenings always did; better in many ways, for a party with the Ashbrooks was as different from the Baxters' as the day was to night. No jockeying for position. No carefully worded compliments and criticisms. No *quid pro quo* underlying every kindness. Merely a meeting of hearts and minds, eager to pass a few hours on a cold winter's night.

Good food, good games, and even better conversation. Charity threw herself into it, forcing herself to focus on the gift of an enjoyable evening, rather than the broken hopes of her heart.

With the new year ushering in, many of their entertainments revolved around predictions for the future, foretelling with total accuracy the wealth and fortune that was to come to each of them in the coming year—including Tabby reading Charity's tea leaves, which prophesied her husband to be an older man with plenty of swagger and a name full of sweetness and flowers.

"As in Honeyfield?" said Charity with an arched brow.

Tabby stared wide-eyed into the cup with far too much innocence to be believed. "I think you may be correct."

Charity glared at her for that, but the lady looked entirely unrepentant before they all shared a laugh and a shudder. No, her future was not tainted by that man, and Charity didn't need tea leaves, cards, or wrinkles on her palms to tell her what was to come.

"It is almost midnight," said Mr. Ashbrook as he rose to his feet.

A maid came forward and passed around glasses of champagne as they joined him in a circle. The others were all paired together, husband and wife, and Charity stood amongst them alone. It didn't matter. It truly didn't. But she couldn't help imagining a certain man standing at her side, gazing at her with that same anticipation as the clock struck twelve.

The group cheered, raising toasts to the old and the new, and soon the first notes of "Auld Lang Syne" rang out. It was such a mournful song that Charity didn't understand why they marked such a festive occasion with such melancholy, but there was something to say about remembering the past and holding it close, despite the march of time dragging you forward. Dredging forth the memories of Old Charity, the New joined in with the rest, singing out the life that was no more; Charity did not wish to return to it, but neither could she erase it. The only way to avoid repeating the past was to remember it, and Charity refused to be that other lady again.

"I am getting too old to stay up all hours of the night," said Mr. Kingsley with a sigh as he set down his glass. "I fear Mina and I must bow out now."

And like the first snowflakes that signaled a flurry, those first farewells drew forth more, and the others followed suit, offering up apologies before gathering their things and heading out into the night. Charity did not want to leave. There was nothing at Juniper Court but an empty house and silent walls, but neither could she impose upon her hosts any longer. Mr. Ashbrook called for her carriage, and Charity bundled herself up, bracing for the coming cold.

At the groom's knock, Charity gave a start; the man was quick about his work, that was for certain. Tugging on her gloves, she opened the door and stopped at the sight of a wet and snow-covered Thomas Callaghan standing on the front steps.

"Hello, Miss Baxter."

Chapter 23

Until that moment, Thomas felt like cursing everyone and everything—the ship that had arrived in port a full fortnight later than intended, the stagecoaches (for there were several) that had gotten themselves stuck in the mud, and the horse who'd decided to throw a shoe, leaving him stranded on an empty stretch of road. Thomas Callaghan felt like a solid block of ice, his greatcoat doing little to stave off the snow and slush that clung to him, and if not for the fact that he was familiar with the signs of frostbite, he would fear for several of his toes.

But standing there with the candlelight from the house bathing his Charity golden light, such mundane frustrations slipped away. Stepping forward, Thomas swept her into his arms just as she threw herself into them.

"I knew it was silly, but I wanted you to come tonight. I wanted it more than anything," she murmured.

Thomas didn't want to put her down, but he longed to see her eyes. The image of them was burned into his memory, but it paled in comparison to seeing them in the flesh, shining in the darkness as Charity gazed at him.

Setting her down, Thomas had every intention of reveling

in the sight of her, but Charity's gaze shone with her heart, making his thump against his ribs. With each beat, it testified that this was the woman who owned it. The one who never allowed him to hide away or pretend, always prodding him to do better as much as she did so for herself. The one who seemed all prickles but only to protect her delicate heart.

The lady who was not content with knowing only a part of him.

Twelve months of surviving on daydreams and letters came crashing down on Thomas, and the last of his willpower evaporated. Capturing her lips, he poured all those months of longing into his touch so that she would know precisely how much he had missed her. Charity's arms came around his neck, pulling him close, and Thomas needed no more prodding. Fire sizzled in his veins until he was certain to melt the snow around them, and his heart thumped erratically, begging him for more and more.

No amount of letters could compensate for touching her, holding her.

"You two are going to catch your death out there," called Graham

That was followed by his wife's sharp whisper, "Hush! Leave them be!"

Charity's eyes snapped open, and she jerked free of Thomas's lips, her brows shooting so high they were liable never to come down again. But he refused to let go of her. His chest rumbled with a laugh, his lips pulling into a smirk.

"You would think a man's closest friend would leave him alone when greeting his lady after twelve months apart," mumbled Thomas.

"You would think a man would know better than to compromise a lady," replied Graham.

Thomas considered that. "Well, if the damage is done..."

He leaned in for another kiss, but Charity huffed and pulled away, her expression telling him to behave (though her gaze promised more sweetnesses to come). Once they were inside the house, Graham gave him a hearty embrace and clapped him on the back.

"I had given up hope you would ever arrive."

Thomas glanced around at the empty parlor. "I see I did so just in time."

But then Mrs. Ashbrook stepped forward and greeted him with a buss. "At least you arrived. I was terrified I would give your secret away."

Charity said nothing, but Thomas caught a look that had him suspecting Mrs. Ashbrook hadn't been as careful as she'd thought.

Then taking his wife by the arm, Graham turned towards the stairs. "The carriage should be here any moment to take Miss Baxter home, but I fear I am done in."

With a sly smile for Thomas, the pair took their leave, and Charity threw herself back into his arms, her own wrapping around his neck.

"I've missed you terribly," she whispered.

Thomas settled his hands at her back, and for the first time, he was entirely uncertain what to say. Words were too trite and simple to convey how much he'd longed for this moment.

"I bought a bottle of your cologne." Charity gave him a wry grin and leaned in, taking a deep breath of him. "It reminded me of you so much that I had to have it. But it never smelled quite the same as it does when you wear it."

"Soaked as I am, I hardly smell of it now."

But Charity nuzzled into his neck, and Thomas held her close, pressing a kiss to her head as she let out a contented sigh. Yes, he wanted to stay in that exact spot forever.

"I've heard of a New Year's tradition that is popular among villages in the north," she whispered, lifting her head to meet his gaze with a laugh sparkling in her eyes. "They say that the first person to cross a threshold after midnight is an omen of what is to come for the year."

Thomas's lips broke into a lazy smile. "I do believe I have heard of that tradition. Isn't it true that a dark-haired fellow with devilish good looks is the best portent?"

"Most certainly," she replied with a grin.

"Well, thank goodness I arrived when I did. Who knows what ill-fortune might've befallen you if I hadn't."

"But this isn't my home, the good fortune you've brought isn't mine."

Thomas balked, his brows raising. "Oh, my dear lady. I fear you've been misinformed. It is not simply the house and family who receive that good fortune, but anyone who was inside when the dark-haired man with the devilish good looks crossed the threshold—which includes you."

Charity gave that a challenging raise of her brow.

"It is the truth," he said with a sharp nod of the head, though Thomas's thoughts grew a little muddled as her fingers tickled his neck, brushing the bare skin at the back of his collar. "And in many traditions, he is supposed to bring gifts that symbolize all the good things to come."

"Ah," she said with a bright smile.

"Unfortunately, I had to leave my bags at the last inn I passed, and they shan't be delivered until tomorrow or the day after," said Thomas with a frown.

"Oh, I am certain there is something you can give me," she whispered, her lips so close they brushed his. Charity's eyes held his, rife with an invitation.

"Is there?" he said with raised brows.

But Charity would have none of his teasing, and she closed the distance again, stealing his breath away. Where the other kiss had been fire and passion stoked by months of longing and waiting, this was born of sweetness and light and of lonely hours wishing for the other, wanting nothing more than to be in their presence. The letters they'd written could fill a novel, but even if they'd written ten times that much, it would never compare to speaking to Charity directly and passing a quiet hour in her company. Listening to her laugh. Seeing her frown when he pestered her.

The sound of the carriage outside had Charity pulling away

with a sigh.

"I am not ready to leave you yet," she whispered. "Now that I've returned, I do not want to be without you—even if it is only for a few hours."

"There is a simple solution to our conundrum," he said with a considering look.

"Which is?" she asked with a raise of her brows.

"Marry me."

Charity jerked back, staring at him. "Pardon?"

"I was near enough to loving you before I left all those months ago, and the mountain of missives has only confirmed it. I adore you, Charity Baxter. I have no choice but to keep sailing for the present, but I cannot bear the thought of leaving the shores before I've made you my wife. For now and for always."

Her hands drifted from his neck to his face, framing his cheeks as she studied him. "You love me?"

"Do you think I go about kissing every woman I meet? I am not that sort of man," he said with mock indignance.

Charity's thumbs brushed against his cheekbones, those eyes searching for who knows what, and Thomas couldn't help but squirm. He'd thought the answer a simple one, but the longer the silence stretched out, the more he felt like pestering her until she answered. But then her lips pressed against his once more, and Thomas found it exceedingly difficult to think of anything but the feel of her in his embrace.

Nothing in the future was certain. Charity had no plans, no expectations. Only questions. So many of them swirled in her mind, all concerning what was to come. But there was one answer she knew and could never doubt. Charity poured the certainty of it in her kiss, hoping her Thomas would know precisely what she wished to say, for she would never be as witty or poetic with her words.

When she released him, Charity reveled in the stupor that had taken hold of him. "How does tomorrow suit you?"

"Pardon?" Thomas's brows rose.

Charity laughed and brushed a soft kiss on his lips. "Shall we marry tomorrow?"

With a chuckle, he shook his head. "I think the vicar may have some strong opinions about the speed with which we may do so, but we can speak to him tomorrow."

"That sounds lovely—" But a horse's whinny drew Charity's gaze to the front windows, and she sighed. "I cannot leave the carriage standing for too long. I fear I must go."

But Thomas did not release his hold of her hand as he swept into a low bow. "It is my gentlemanly duty to escort you home, my lady, to protect you from highwaymen and brigands and any other dangers that lurk in the darkness."

"Is that so?"

Holding her gaze, he pressed a kiss to her palm. "It is my honor."

Straightening, Thomas wove her hand through his arm and led her into the night. Though darkness surrounded them, the brightness of her joy filled the world with light, chasing away the shadows of the past and leaving Charity in no doubt that their future was bright.

Whatever may come, they would sort it out. Together.

Exclusive Offer

Join the M.A. Nichols VIP Reader Club at

www.ma-nichols.com

to receive up-to-date information about upcoming books, freebies, and VIP content!

About the Author

Born and raised in Anchorage, M.A. Nichols is a lifelong Alaskan with a love of the outdoors. As a child she despised reading but through the love and persistence of her mother was taught the error of her ways and has had a deep, abiding relationship with it ever since.

She graduated with a bachelor's degree in landscape management from Brigham Young University and a master's in landscape architecture from Utah State University, neither of which has anything to do with why she became a writer, but is a fun little tidbit none-the-less. And no, she doesn't have any idea what type of plant you should put in that shady spot out by your deck. She's not that kind of landscape architect. Stop asking.

Website | Facebook | Instagram | BookBub

Printed in Great Britain
by Amazon

35805633R00097